The Heart Hath Its Reasons

Catholic Novella
in Sundry Shades of Love
(Ordered and Otherwise)

by

Bernard Scott

LOGOS INSTITUTE PRESS

Other Books by the Author

Secret of Lost Mountain
(short novel)

Brian's Law
(short stories)

The Mystery of Work
(anthology)

*The Redeemer's Call to
Consecrated Souls*
(translation from the French)

The Logos Story
(forthcoming)

Language, Brains and the Computer
(forthcoming)

ISBN 978 - 0980117493

LOGOS INSTITUTE PRESS
TARPON SPRINGS, FL 34689

logos.institute@gmail.com

To my spiritual father who
commissioned me to
write about love

To my wife, Arlene, whose love
made it possible

THE HEART HATH ITS REASONS

THAT REASON KNOWETH NOT

—BLAISE PASCAL

SUNDRY SHADES OF LOVE

THE CLEANING LADY

THE CLEANING WOMAN WAS LATE. She was new and I had to delay leaving for the office until she arrived. It wasn't long though before I heard her voice out in the hallway inquiring for my apartment. I noted it sounded pleasant. Judging from the voice, I figured a woman maybe in her late twenties. I wondered whether she would be attractive. Something in her voice made me think of it. Would a good-looking woman clean apartments for a living? Such things happen.

The doorbell rang, and I went to let her in. The woman who stood before me was maybe thirty but I could not take my eyes from her face. I tried not to do this, for others all her life must have had the same reaction. It wasn't that she was ugly exactly, not at all, but it would be fair to say the face was unfortunate. Yet something about her seemed nice enough.

"Ah, Miss Gramercy," I said. "Or is it Mrs.?"

"Oh, no," she said. Then she added, with a lilting laugh, "Not yet!" I decided she could be well under thirty. It was hard to tell with a face like that. Her voice had a

1

nice little ring to it though. I felt right away she'd do just fine.

I led her in and began showing her around the place. "It's a mess, I know," I said.

"It's no different than other men like yourself," she said pleasantly.

"Have you done other single guys?" I asked, looking at my watch. I might still make that meeting.

"Oh, I only do men's places," she answered, opening the door to my office. That was rather bold of her, I reflected, taking the door from her.

"I keep this room closed," I said. "Organized chaos. If you touch anything, I'm lost."

She picked up a necktie of mine lying there on the floor, something I had ruined the other night at an Italian restaurant.

"I meant to throw that out," I said, taking it from her and tossing it into the wastebasket. "My Italian designer tie," I said with half a laugh.

"It's all right," she said, "I understand."

She looked around her. "Fifty dollars," she said.

"Good," I said, "You have yourself a client." I looked at my watch again.

"When can you start?" I asked her.

"Whenever you like," she said. "I can start tomorrow, Thursday."

"Wonderful! Terrific! Thursdays. The key will be under the mat outside the door. Just leave it on the table when you go. I'm out of here by eight-thirty so the place is yours any time after that."

"I like to start early," she said. She poked her head into a closet.

"No closets," I said. "Just the open rooms, okay?"

"Of course, Mr. Kwiatk . . . ," she hesitated. No one can ever pronounce my last name, not unless you're Polish,

"Just call me Jan," I said. I reached into my office for my briefcase.

"Mr. Jan," she repeated with that nice ring.

She preceded me down the hall towards the front door. From behind you'd never think she was hard to look at. I like to try to figure out what a woman looks like from what you could observe walking behind her, sort of the way paleontologists reconstruct some prehistoric creature from nothing more than a hipbone. It works for everything but the face. The face is always a surprise. I noticed, though, that she had a nice light step, almost like a dancer's.

"Well, Ms. Gramercy," I said, opening the front door for her, "if you have any questions or anything just leave me a note with the key. I'll leave the check there also. I'll make it out to cash. Guess that's everything," I said, stepping out into the hall with her. "Yes, I'm leaving too," I said when she seemed surprised. "I'd offer to drop you, but I'm terribly late."

I went ahead down the hall and as I turned towards the elevators, I saw her still standing there looking at me. Strange duck, I thought, and then put her out of my mind entirely. I was having Monica over for drinks tomorrow night and for once the place would look decent.

3

Let me tell you about Monica. She works for the same company I do, in marketing. Monica is what you would have to call "together." She's got it all, and no bones about it, she knows it. Fab looks, smart, confident, with a keen eye for whatever will do Monica some good. Monica is going places. Monica lets no moss grow under her nifty feet, with their slim ankles and you name it from there on up. Now don't get me wrong. She has a soft vulnerable side too, sort of. Yesterday she came into my office and broke into tears. Charlie Boyers, marketing VP, had just met her in the hall and told her she ought to learn how to spell. Didn't she know the Brits use *s* instead of *z*? The Brits of course were all smiles and condescension, but far as he was concerned, the British Airways presentation had been a disaster. Actually it wasn't Monica's doing that merchandise was misspelled with a *z*, even in American English. Boyers never caught the irony. But that's the trouble with groupware, and Monica was taking the rap. You can believe that gal doesn't suffer such things lightly. That's why I asked her over for drinks, or one of the reasons. I thought she could use some building up. We all need stroking from time to time, right?

I'd had my eye on Monica ever since she came with the company, for one thing because we both have the kind of Polish last names you need help with, and even then, good luck. People used to come up to me and ask how to pronounce hers. When I got to know her, she let on she first became aware of me for the same reason. But her surname is beyond impossible, I must say. And she likes it that way.

She's plenty spunky, and I take to women like that, up to a point anyway. And she's something else to look at, like some model out of a glossy brochure for fancy luggage. Like I said, a woman going places.

We couldn't have dinner out that night because Monica goes to school late on Thursday evenings. She's got a year left for her MBA in market chaos theory. But she came over right from class.

"You hungry?" I asked.

"Famished, but I'm being good," she said, brushing her hair back from her face. She wore her hair loose and was always doing something with it. "Whatcha got?" she said flopping onto the sofa. "I am really strung out."

"How about some smoked white fish? And a nice quiet Chablis."

"Absolutely," she said, looking around. I could tell she saw at once the place had been straightened up. A guy would never notice something like that.

I got stuff out of the fridge and set the Chablis and some glasses on the coffee table.

Monica had been to my place often enough before so there was no need to stand on formalities. Not that we were involved with each other, but we weren't what you'd call at arm's length either. "Free spirits" is probably the word. But the truth is I hardly knew Monica. I liked her a lot, though, and was curious to know what she was like behind all that frontal effort of hers.

I opened the wine bottle and half-filled the glasses. "Cheers," I said holding up my glass. Monica glanced at her wine and went for the food instead.

"I had a few words with Boyers today," she said, munching on some fish.

"Did you straighten him out?" I asked.

"Rath-er," she said, reaching for the wine. "In my inimitable way, of course," she added.

"Really?" I said. You never had to lead Monica conversationally.

"Really," she said, sweeping her hair back. "I told him his spelling remark was uncalled for, for one thing, and counterfactual for another. He should know I used to cream my grade school spelling bees year after year. I was a district finalist one year, for god's sake."

"No kidding," I said. The difficulties with her boss didn't interest me all of a sudden. "How's grad school?" I said after an off-kilter pause.

"Don't ask," she said. "Unless you can tell me what the derivational coefficient of the epsilon decay factor is good for."

"Got me," I said.

"Me too," she said, and laughed.

We listened to some cool minimalist jazz after that. A new disk by the black pianist, Chestnut, doing a riff with a Brazilian guitarist whose name I can't remember. Very nice stuff. Monica liked it too. I sat across from her, and we just put our heads back, closed our eyes, and forgot the world for a while. I liked being with her that way.

"This is nice," I said, looking over at her.

"Yes," she replied. She was studying the far wall. Then she said, "I notice you've changed your watercolors around."

I swung around to see what she meant. It was true. They were three watercolors I'd gotten on the Côte d'Azur two summers ago. One was a large study of an old woman tending an immense rose bush. And two smaller ones showed some children playing with rose petals that had fallen at her feet. The roses were pure white. But the arrangement of the three pictures was different. The cleaning woman must have re-hung them when she dusted them. Strange thing for her to do.

"They work better that way," Monica said. "I like that lady," she added wistfully, gesturing toward the larger watercolor. "Reminds me of my grandmother."

"I was right there when the artist was painting it," I said. "The one on the right. Young guy. He was doing the petals. Just a flick of the brush and he had it. Talk about free."

She looked at her watch. "Am I going home tonight?" she asked.

"Whatever you'd like," I said. I must have flushed a little. Monica was all business. Too cut and dried at times.

She studied me for a moment. "Tell me," she said. "Do you think I was too hard on Boyers? You've known him longer than I have."

"Naw," I said. "He's all right. He can take it, just like he can give it out. You don't have to worry."

"I'm not worried," she corrected me. "I just don't want to, you know, alienate anyone."

"No problem," I said. "Every day's a new day with Charlie. He's already forgotten it."

There was a silence. "Why not stay?" I said. "I have a new CD . . ."

"Better not, not tonight," she said getting up. "To tell you the truth, I'm really beat." She looked at me sweetly. "Next time, okay? Come to my place. I'll even cook."

I saw her out to the elevators. We got in a quick kiss as the elevator arrived. "Bye," she said. She gave me a big smile just as the doors closed.

Back in my place I stood before the watercolors. They did look better, come to think of it. But what a thing to do! I'd have to watch this cleaning woman. She was turning out to be quite an original.

I did not expect to be running into Ms. Gramercy anytime soon again so when she turned up next Thursday before I left for work, I didn't know whether to be annoyed or amused. I was still in my T-shirt. Original is not the word for her. And I had forgotten how homely she was. Well, maybe "homely" is not quite the right word, but it's close.

She had brought some bagels and cream cheese. She went right for the kitchen and put them on the table. I noticed the cream cheese was veggie and low fat, exactly the kind I buy myself.

"That your lunch or what?" I said.

"I know you like whole wheat," she said. "And you're on a diet." She began cutting the bagel.

I didn't have to ask how she knew all that. I could just see her sticking that mug of hers into my fridge going through everything there, item by item. Was she some kind of creep?

"Ms. Gramercy," I said, "I've been meaning to ask you. Why did you change my watercolors around like that?"

"Should I make coffee?" she asked. She went to the cupboard where I keep the decaffeinated beans.

"Please answer my question," I said. "That was a strange thing for you to do, don't you think? To change a guy's furnishings around like that."

"You didn't like it?" she asked, turning around to look at me.

"Well, it's not that. I just want to know why did you do it?"

"You didn't like it," she repeated, her face showing alarm.

"No, it's fine," I said. "It's fine. I just felt it was unusual for you to do that, I mean. Don't you think?"

She brushed her hair back. Sort of the way Monica does. "I didn't mind," she said. "I could see you hadn't thought much about how those pictures should go." She began grinding the beans.

I shrugged and went back to the bedroom to finish dressing. When I returned, the coffee was perked and a single bagel, sliced with a modest layer of cream cheese, sat on the kitchen table next to my favorite coffee mug. The cleaning lady herself was in the guest bathroom. I could hear her flushing out the toilet bowl. At least she's not expecting to have breakfast with me, I realized with half-amused relief. I poured coffee and gobbled down half a bagel standing up. I grabbed my briefcase and made for the door. As I went out I caught the cleaning lady standing at the other end of the living room watching me. I saw

9

something pass across that incredible face of hers, something I'm not sure I can name. Nothing you'd expect in a cleaning lady, that's for sure.

I ran into Charlie Boyers later that morning in the men's room. He and I had come into the company around the same time, at the same level. He'd gotten promoted twice since, but we were still pretty friendly.

"Kwaty," he said, his klutzy nickname for me from the first two bastardized syllables of my last name. "I just had some interesting words with your comrade-in-arms." He looked under the stalls.

"My comrade-in-arms," I repeated flatly. I liked giving him a hard time.

"Oh, come on," he said impatiently. He shook his head, "I can't make her out."

"I heard about it," I said with a chuckle.

"You heard?" Charlie was staring right at me, a big frown pasted across his face.

"Well, she mentioned something about the Brits. You know, the spelling."

"Oh, that, I'm not talking about that. This is something else. She's a hot ticket," he said.

I smiled. "She's got what it takes."

"Loaded for bear," he said. He looked under the stall doors again. He drew close and lowered his voice. "She practically propositioned me," he said with a funny look. "Just now, in the goddam elevator."

I looked at him with eyes that must have grown twice their normal size.

"You serious?" I said, adding, "I find that hard to believe."

"Thanks a lot," he said with that toss of his head. "I should report her," he joked. "Reverse harassment. Somebody could make some money."

We both laughed over that one. "What'd she say?" I asked.

Charlie drew close and was about to drop his little bombshell when someone came into the men's room. He made a face.

"I'll see you later about that, old Buddy," he said aloud as he left. "Drop by my office."

I nodded and washed my hands. I never did go to see Charlie. I want to think he made a mistake. Maybe he doesn't appreciate Monica's ironic streak. But you never know. Monica is the kind of woman who's capable of anything, I suppose. Whatever it takes. Who knows? There were some things I'd just as soon stay ignorant of. Must have an old-fashioned streak, a hangover from my parochial school nuns, probably.

We had an interdepartmental meeting that afternoon and both Monica and Charlie were there. Those two exchanged ideas like nothing in the world had gone on between them. We were all the perfect professionals. All business. Squeaky clean. People should know the things that go on. Maybe Monica's right. Irony's what keeps a dull world interesting. She's a trip all right.

Things went along in my life fairly smooth for a time. As it turned out the company got the British Airways account. Something else Monica had worked on drew favorable mention from the Brits so she was in seventh heaven for days on end. We had dinner twice over that, but always out. Monica wasn't exactly my girlfriend, and she had other guys she saw, so who was I to expect special treatment? But I liked her, and I wouldn't mind if the relationship started to go somewhere. I brought it up during dinner one night.

"Everything good now between you and Boyers?" I asked stirring my coffee.

"I can't figure him out," she said, pushing her hair back with that sudden gesture of hers. "I should tell you some of the things he says to me . . . between the lines," she added with a quick glance in my direction. "You wouldn't believe."

"Yeah, Charlie's a sketch," I said with a weak enough laugh. I suddenly realized that most of the time with Monica she doesn't look at you. And when she does, she's talking about herself and wants to get your reaction.

She leaned toward me and lowered her voice. "He wants me to go to the Chicago convention with him."

"With him?" I repeated.

"Well, you know, with his team," she said leaning back. "Why would he ask me? I've never gone to this thing before."

"Looks like somebody's moving up," I said with an attempt at the positive side.

"He took me aside last week to talk to me about it," she said. She was looking down at her wine glass and began to twirl it thoughtfully. I reached for the bottle and began to pour.

She put out her hand to signal enough. "He told me he put me in for a merit raise," she said.

"Hey, honey, I didn't come here to talk about Charlie Boyers," I said with I guess barely hidden exasperation. "Let's talk about us."

"You brought him up," she said.

"Yeah," I said. "Good old Charlie. He's probably got the hots for you."

"I thought we were going to change the subject," Monica said looking around for the waiter. "I'd like more coffee," she said, looking back at me.

"What's with us, do you think?" I started. "Are we going any place together?"

She smiled. "What do you mean?"

"You know what I'm saying," I said. She was looking at me like she saw me for the first time that night.

"Come on, you know what I mean."

"What did you have in mind," she asked, laughing. "Côte d'Azur?"

I laughed a little too. "Why not," I said. "That's not a bad idea actually. We get away from the rat race; we really get to know each other. Two weeks of unbroken bliss. Just you and me, perfect together." Then I added with a mock bow, "And a fresh white rose delivered every morning with breakfast. One for each of us. From the old woman on my wall."

"You're such a dreamer," she said. Then she said, "If I'm going to stay at your place tonight, I've got to have some strong black coffee. I need to put this headache to bed first. It's been that kind of day for me, believe me."

13

I woke up about seven-thirty the next morning. Monica was already in the bathroom. I could hear the hair blower. Then it hit me like a ton of bricks. It was Thursday, and the cleaning lady was due to arrive in a half an hour, less even. She'd even been coming before eight. Half the time I'd make it a point to get out of the house by then and have my breakfast in a coffee shop just to avoid her. What can you say to a cleaning lady who keeps wanting to do something nice for you? What does she want from me? It's all these little things she does. You hardly notice, but they're there. I keep pistachios in a little bowl by the TV, for example. I like pistachios. So do most of my friends. We can overdose on them during a good game. I keep a supply in a tin on my kitchen shelf. Would you believe that in three months the level in that tin has never changed. Not since she started coming here. Just like that miraculous cruse of oil in Greek mythology, or the Bible, or whatever. The goddam thing is always filled right where it was the day she came here. It's weird. I only pay her for half a day, mind you, but the doorman tells me she doesn't leave 'til just before I get home from work. She's here all day, every Thursday. Going through my stuff probably. Who knows what she knows about me by this time. She knows where things are better than I do. Last week I was getting ready to leave for the office, and I couldn't find my car keys. She knew where they were. That same morning when I was going out the door she spoke my first name, without the "Mister." When I turned around, there she was again at the far end of the living room, looking at me like a wife seeing her husband off. "I

14

hope you have a good day today," she said in that lilting voice of hers. Then her face brightened into this big smile, like she had gotten something off her chest. You know, the truth is she's nice actually, or tries to be. If only she had another face—one you could keep looking at without, you know, wishing it was something else.

Monica came into the bedroom, still draped in a towel. "Forget the white rose," she said. "Coffee will do just fine." Then she put out her arms and said playfully, "Oh, don't get up. Allow me." She padded down the hall and I could soon hear her rattling things in the kitchen. Monica's about as undomesticated as you can get. I went into the shower. It was almost quarter to eight. Whatever happens about the cleaning lady would just have to happen.

The doorbell rang as I was stepping out of the shower. "Monica," I called down the hall, "it's the cleaning lady. Just let her in."

I heard the front door open and close, and a few seconds later Monica came down the hall. She was still draped in a towel, barefoot.

"She's going to make the coffee," Monica said, heading back to the bathroom.

So there we were. The two women in my life. My would-be girlfriend and my strange-duck cleaning lady. Monica and I sat down at the kitchen table with two place settings today. In the middle were some scones. I felt them to see that they were still warm. Some time ago I decided I liked warm scones for breakfast, right from the bakery—when I could get them, that is. On Thursdays. The coffee too was all poured, waiting for us. The cleaning

15

lady had gone to the back of the apartment. She was probably changing the bed. I had her doing that now, too.

"Where'd you get her?" Monica asked, dipping a scone into her coffee.

"Some agency," I said.

"She's cute," Monica said.

"Yeah, cute," I said.

"No, I mean she's very nice," she said. "It's hard to find someone good anymore."

I felt depressed. Somehow I didn't relish having these two women here at the same time. Some things you never mix, like pickles and cream or something.

"It's late. We'd better go," I said.

"I forgot my jacket," Monica said. She didn't have to go back to the bedroom for it. My cleaning lady suddenly appeared with it on her arm.

"You'll want this, Miss."

"Oh yeah, thanks," Monica said giving her a really big smile.

The cleaning lady just looked at her for a moment and said nothing. Then she turned to me. "Mr. Jan," she said, "May I speak with you? I have to tell you something."

"Is it important?" I said. "We're running late."

"It will only take a minute," she said.

"I'll meet you in the garage," Monica said as she headed for the door.

I looked at the cleaning lady. "She's a good friend," I said as Monica left.

"Yes," she said. After a moment, she added, "I hope you and she will be happy."

16

"Well, thanks," I said, "but it's not what you think."

"Mr. Jan, this will be my last day," she announced suddenly.

"Hey, listen," I said. "I'm not leaving here. Did you think that . . . " I stopped. I didn't have to explain my life to her. If she leaves that's her business.

I grabbed my things. "I really don't have time to talk to you about it. Is it the money?"

"No," she said. She saw that I was leaving and began to follow me.

"Oh, god," I said. "I forgot the check." I hesitated at the door. "Listen, I'll send it to you. Leave your address on the mantel with the key, okay?"

I stopped in the doorway and looked back at her. She had turned her back to me. I had the feeling she was crying. "Ms. Gramercy," I said. She heard me because she turned her head slightly, but she wouldn't look at me. "Look," I said, "I don't want you to leave. You know I'm very satisfied with your service. I'll give you an increase. Come back next Thursday and we can talk about it. Over scones," I said, trying a laugh. She just hung her head, her back still to me, and shook it from side to side ever so slowly.

I have to tell you that I sort of miss that woman. I didn't realize what she had been doing for me until I saw that I started running out of soap, nuts, you name it. Her name was Maryann. I found that out the next Thursday when I got, would you believe it, a white rose delivered with a note with just her name on it. Maryann Gramercy. The weirdest thing was that there was one for Monica too, labeled "For her." That woman must have no life. I

17

don't know, she was so . . . well, let's just say she wasn't easy to look at.

But this isn't the way it ended. Not entirely. One morning a few months later, as I was waiting for the elevator, late for work, the elevator doors opened and some guy got off carrying this little package. He looked around like he wasn't sure where to go. Is that for six? I asked. The guy shoved the package at me and grabbed the elevator back down. He was in even more of a hurry than I was. I looked at the sender's name: Maryann Parks. I didn't know any Parks. Maryann . . . The face of the cleaning lady popped into mind. Sure, and it was Thursday. And it was her funny little handwriting . . . Parks . . . Some guy saw something in her after all.

I was really late now so I just stuffed the package into my pocket. It was soft, but whatever it was could wait. On a late morning like that I would normally be hopping it to my Beamer in the garage, but for some stupid reason I stopped. I had to open the package. There was no note or anything. What I found inside was my necktie, that old Italian designer job of mine, the one with the tomato stains, the one I tossed into the wastebasket that first morning she came. I couldn't believe it. The spots were gone. She'd had the bloody thing cleaned.

GREATLY REDUCED

CHARLIE BOYERS WASN'T TERRIBLY OVERWEIGHT but he was flabby, and he had a beer belly. And he was big to start with. Being big and flabby was a bad combination, bad for one's image at the office, to say nothing of one's self-image. No one would guess Charlie Boyers harbored negative feelings about himself—he was confidence personified. Nevertheless a tremor of impending disaster had now registered itself someplace in his thirty-six-year-old gray matter.

It started the morning he stepped out of the shower and, as he reached for a towel, he saw his dripping, naked body in the full-length mirror. The sight of all that flesh made him wince. Maybe it was the way he was bending over with his stomach hanging down like that, like some pregnant woman. He stood up and let his stomach muscles hang out. The man in the mirror was a stranger. This wasn't the Charlie Boyers in his head. He straightened up, wrapped the towel tightly around him and drew himself back into shape, more or less. But it had registered. Things about him had changed right underneath his nose, while he wasn't looking, so to speak.

The Charlie Boyers of the mind had assumed its final definitive form about ten years ago, around the time of his first big promotion. He had been out of college a few years, was working hard, was well-liked at the office, and was going to the athletic club every day at lunch to work out with the guys.

The break for him came when the marketing vice-president began looking for him to play racket-ball. Charlie Boyers was six feet three, had a big reach and played hard. He had been a defensive lineman at Cornell, not a starter, but he got to play. The image of himself ten years ago was a defining one for Charlie Boyers, and he held onto it. This was who he was—lean, hard working, sort of easy-going with maybe a flinty edge hinted at, generally well-regarded, no negatives anybody could point to. Eminently promotable, in other words. That was him. But then he got his second promotion, and Charlie stopped going to the athletic club. Lunches were for business, and the thought of going to the club evenings was a nice idea but couldn't compete with the comforts of home and a wife.

That was years ago, so when he told his wife the other day that he had rejoined the club and would be coming home late two nights a week, she understood her husband was probably entering the proverbial mid-life crisis a little early. Her friend Nancy said it was bound to happen and told her what to expect. "They start noticing their body," she said. "Then they start noticing your body," she added. "That's when they start looking around."

Margaret, Charlie Boyers' wife, wasn't too concerned. She looked good, and she knew it. She didn't have to work at it either; nature had been good to her. She wasn't worried about Charlie that way anyway. Things had gradually cooled off, but that was natural. They weren't kids anymore, and Charlie could stand to lose a little. And he could take his son along. Their Billy could stand to lose a little weight as well.

"Ask your father if you can go with him," she said to her son one evening. It was one of the nights that Charlie was having dinner at the club before working out.

"Mom, I got too much to do," Billy said.

"Ask him," his mother said. "He'd love it. Besides you could stand to lose a little."

"Hasn't made a dent on Dad," Billy said.

"It takes time," his mother said.

But when the subject was brought up one night as they were going to bed, Charlie made a little face and wiggled out of it. "Billy wouldn't enjoy it," Charlie said. "Lot of rough talk—you know how it is with the guys sometimes. Besides, I'd have to come home and get Billy and, what with the traffic and everything, it wouldn't work out."

"Well, it would do you both some good," Margaret said. "You don't spend much time with him."

"Hey, is that my fault? You got him doing his music thing all the time. I couldn't even take him hunting."

"He's not the type."

21

"Yeah, right," Charlie said. "And he's not going to take to pumping iron either. You want his muscles to be supple."

"He could swim," Margaret said.

"You know I hate water," Charlie said.

That's how it ended, but Margaret noticed something new. When Charlie went to bed that night he didn't touch her once.

Charlie actually began to trim down over the next weeks and was starting to look good. But Margaret noticed he seemed tired when he came home those nights, and before long usually headed straight for bed, falling asleep before she even joined him. Margaret attributed it to his being out of shape, but Nancy disagreed.

"It doesn't surprise me," she said. "He's starting to live his own life in his own world. You'll see."

Margaret paid no attention. Nancy had had three husbands and didn't trust men. It was different with Margaret. She and her husband were different types, true enough, but they were good friends.

But Nancy knew what she was talking about. Charlie had gotten in with some guys about his age, all doing the same thing, reaching back for something they didn't want to lose. But it wasn't the guys that kept him out so late. It was that good-looker from the office.

"Hey, look who's here," Charlie said when he saw her at the pool. Mondays, Wednesdays and Fridays the pool was co-ed, and so before long Charlie was going to the club three nights a week.

"First it's two nights, now it's three nights," Nancy commented when Margaret told her what was happening.

"He's lost a lot of weight," Margaret said. "He looks good."

"Sure," Nancy said, "he's shed the pounds. Now what else will he shed?"

Margaret didn't like that kind of talk, but she felt she had to take a stand. "Charlie," she said one night as they were watching television, "are you going hunting with the fellows again this year?"

"Not sure, maybe," Charlie said, not taking his eyes off the tube.

"I was thinking," Margaret said, "maybe you could take Billy with you this time."

"Him go hunting?" Charlie said, looking over at his wife.

"He would like it," she said.

"He didn't the last time," Charlie said with a face.

"He'd like being with you," she said.

"Yeah," Charlie said, looking back at the screen.

"Sally and Joe invited us over for dinner this Friday," she said.

"Friday? Why Friday? That's my night at the Club."

"Does it matter to miss one night?" she said. "You've already lost plenty."

"I don't like to break the rhythm."

"Go Thursday. What's the difference."

"Yeah," he said. He got up and turned the TV off.

"Is something wrong?"

"It's a stupid show," he said, heading for the kitchen.

23

"Why do they put stuff like that on anymore?"

"Charlie," she said, following him. "Billy would really like to go."

"Did he say that?" Charlie said.

"No, but I know he would. He doesn't get to see you that much."

"Yeah," Charlie said, opening a can of beer. "I'd take him hunting. You bet I would. But you got him into this crazy Suzuki thing."

"He loves playing the violin," she said. "Besides, you used to play the piano."

Charlie looked at his wife. "You want to know something, Margaret. I think *you* love his playing. I listen to him," he added with a face.

"His teacher says he has talent."

"Yeah, sure, why wouldn't she, for forty bucks an hour."

Margaret took Charlie's hand. "Honey, he's your son."

"I'm sorry, sweet," he said putting the beer down. "If I go this year I'll take him . . . If he wants."

"Thanks, honey," she said with a big smile. "You're a darling."

And that night things went better.

"You're wrong, Nancy," Margaret told her friend the next day. "Nothing has changed."

Nancy frowned. "Margaret, I didn't want to tell you this. But he's seeing someone."

"I don't believe it," Margaret said. "How can you say such a thing?"

Nancy shook her head. "I have a friend who goes to

the club. She's seen them together."

"What? What are you saying?" Margaret said. "Seen who together?"

"Your husband and some girl almost half his age," she said. "They hang out together at the pool."

"I don't believe you," Margaret said. "I know Charlie. He doesn't like the water."

"Okay," Nancy said, "don't take my word for it. You'll find out."

That night when Charlie got home from the club, his wife asked him about the pool. "Someone saw you at the pool the other day," she said.

"Really?" he said. "Who was that?"

"I thought you didn't like water," she said.

"I don't go in," he said. "You know I don't swim."

Margaret remained silent.

"I have friends at the club," he said. "They like the pool. One of them is from the office."

"Is one of them a girl?" she asked.

"Is that what your gossip told you?" he said, smirking.

Margaret looked down. A tear had formed in her eyes.

"Honey," he said. "It's not what you think. Believe me."

But after that, Charlie stopped going to the club. When Margaret related that to Nancy, Nancy had something else to tell her. "My friend has seen them having lunch together. You'll see."

It's true that relations between Charlie and his wife began to cool. When she mentioned it to him, he said all these suspicions about him turned him off. She never mentioned she knew about the lunches. Maybe, she figured, there weren't lunches, only lunch, one lunch. Gossip is such poison.

"Is Charlie taking Billy with him hunting this year?" Nancy asked the next time they were together.

Margaret shook her head. "Charlie didn't go this year," she said sadly.

"He always goes hunting," she said. "Like a ritual."

"Yes," Margaret said.

"He's changing," Nancy said. "Just like all of them. Is he staying late at the office?"

"Sometimes," Margaret said. "But he doesn't go to the club anymore."

"That's something," Nancy said.

"And he still looks good," Margaret said. "He lost a lot of weight."

Nancy took her friend's hand. "Honey, do yourself a favor. Get yourself a sign. 'Soon-to-be-former husband for sale. Greatly reduced.'"

"No," Margaret said, shuddering. "Don't even think that."

"I hate to say it," Nancy said. "Men are men. You'll see. By the way, her name is Monica—just so you know."

HOMILY FOR ONE

THE YOUNG PAROCHIAL VICAR, Father Timothy O'Brian, charged into the rectory kitchen of St. Andrew's and stamped the morning snow off his feet. The wind had slammed the door shut behind him, occasioning an unpriestly crack about the building committee years ago that decided priests could well do without a covered passageway. It was only thirty yards from the church where he had just said the seven-thirty.

He hung up his coat as his superior, Father Louis Reilly, St. Andrew's pastor, chuckled, "There's fresh, hot coffee, Tim, and oatmeal on the stove."

"Just what I wanted," the younger priest said making a face.

"Goes with the weather," Father Louis said with a grin.

Father Tim dutifully dished out some of the thick gruel his boss had prepared. The two priests sat facing each other listening to the wind outside. It was seven-fifty and the worst storm of the winter was full upon them, so fierce even their faithful housekeeper, Martha, did not show up.

"Anybody there this morning?" Father Louis asked.

"Just that young woman," Father Tim said. "You know, the looker who's been coming the last few weeks. The one who sits in the back and never receives. I hear she's got a doozy of a last name. Polish, I'm told. "

"Ah, yes," Father Louis said, "She's been coming to the nine o'clock. I have no idea who she is."

"Well, storm or no storm, she got up for the seven-thirty this morning," Father Tim said, slapping beads of melting snow from his pant leg. "She followed me into the sacristy with a smart question."

"Well, at least she listens," Fr. Louis said, adding coffee to their mugs.

"Yeah, well today," his young assistant said, "it was the words in the Antiphon: *In love he created us, in justice he condemned us, in mercy he restored us to life.* She stuck her face in the sacristy after Mass and wanted to know if God is so loving and merciful, why did He have to condemn us? She just stood there until I gave her an answer. I sure wouldn't want to be married to this one."

"So what did you tell her?" Father Louis said smiling.

"I told her she'd asked a good question," Father Tim said.

The older priest finished off his coffee. "I suppose that's one way to handle it," he said.

Father Louis got up and put his mug in the sink. He listened to a gust of wind slam against the kitchen window.

"By the way," he asked as he turned to go. "Did you give a homily?"

"Never for one," Father Tim said with a laugh. "Against my religion."

"You might have a point," the pastor said, heading for his office.

Father Louis had the nine o'clock. The wind and snow were snarling more than ever as he fought across the yards to the church, entering by the rear sacristy door. He brushed himself off and quickly robed in the green vestments of Ordinary Time. He poked his head out into the half-darkened church. It looked empty, as he expected. He would only need lights over the altar, but some movement in the back told him he was mistaken. The priest peered out into the dimly lit nave and saw the lone figure of a woman seated far in the back. He was sure it was her. He snapped on a few additional lights and then, giving a few tugs on the warning bell, went out to the altar.

As he approached the altar steps, he saw that the girl in the back did not rise. An angry Catholic, he reflected. Or maybe not Catholic at all. Going up to the altar he wished he hadn't made that judgment. It didn't matter. The Mass was for everyone, for the whole world, good and bad, maybe even least of all for the good. But in another moment Father Louis forgot about the girl, forgot about everything but the words he began to intone, words he recited every day of his priesthood, without fail, and knew he would recite until the day he died: *Lord have mercy,*

Christ have mercy, Lord have mercy. It was what he was there for, to say these same words day after day, and hope—no, *believe* they made a difference. *Help thou my unbelief.* This cry from Scripture was also his. He would not care to admit to anyone how often these words flashed through his mind.

The Gospel he read aloud that morning was from *Matthew*, where Jesus issues one of his dire "gnashing of teeth" warnings:

> *The kingdom of heaven is like a net which was thrown into the sea and gathered fish of every kind; when it was full, men drew it ashore and sat down and sorted the good into the vessels but threw away the bad. So it will be at the close of the age. The angels will come out and separate the evil from the righteous, and throw them into the furnace of fire; there will be weeping and gnashing of teeth.*

Father Louis was half-inclined not to deliver a homily for one person either, but somehow changed his mind, and as he closed the Lectionary, he began to talk about hell. The words he spoke actually surprised him, for it was not a topic he had ever touched on. It was not a long homily, just a few stark sentences like the shafts of wind that morning that every few seconds pounded the stained glass windows lining the walls of the church. Hearing his voice bounce off the empty pews, he wondered if he was just talking to himself.

"We have to understand," he said, "that there is a hell. We may not like it, but there it is, like it or not. We

30

don't know who is in hell of course, or if anyone at all is in hell gnashing their teeth. But it is very likely hell is well-populated. Sin that's serious, if it isn't repented, separates us from God, and hell is that separation for all eternity. So, if there is sin, there is hell. You can't have one without the other. And, God knows, there is sin. There is something greater than sin and hell, to be sure, and that's God's mercy. Let us never forget that. And let us hope hell is empty. But we should stop and ask ourselves what possible meaning can mercy have if there is no hell."

After Father Louis spoke these words he sat down. The church seemed to echo with silence. The only sounds were the windows along the walls complaining of harsh, bitter wind. He liked to be quiet after the homily, a few unhurried moments when nothing had to happen. Already too long for some. The grumblers. But he knew there were others, others who in those moments felt peace settling in, and he offered that silence for them. But today, his eyes closed, Father Louis felt none of that peace himself. He was already unsure he should have said those words. What had gotten into him? He had never talked about hell. Must be this weather, he reflected, or maybe this shadowy woman in the back of the church. You never know. Strange how he could feel her fighting every word he spoke.

Father Louis offered the sacrifice of the Mass and consumed the sacred species. He held the paten in his hand with a single host and waited a few moments just in case. When the woman made no move to come forward, he turned to the tabernacle and placed the host in the

31

ciborium, saying a prayer for her, then he purified the chalice and gave the final blessing.

Stepping down from the altar he went quickly into the sacristy and began unvesting. Pulling the alb over his head and looking up, it came as no great surprise to find her standing there in the doorway watching him. Father Louis had to agree with his associate—the young lady certainly was attractive, all wrapped up in a lush, cashmere coat.

"I have some problems with your sermon," she said. She reached up and drew the cashmere closer about her.

Father Louis chuckled. "I can understand why."

"I don't believe in hell," she said.

Father Louis opened a closet door and hung up his alb. "It doesn't matter what we believe, you know," he said, shutting the door. "God doesn't ask for our opinions." He smiled at her as he reached for his overcoat and snapped out all the lights but one in the very back of the church. Some of the gloom outside seeped back into the empty, unlit nave.

"I have to lock the doors," he said, making a move to the rear of the church.

She stood in his way. "Why does God have to punish anyone?" she said. "Forever and ever, just because you made a mistake?"

Father Louis waited until she stepped aside. "I don't think He does," he said, "not for a mistake."

The young woman followed him through the semi-darkness to the back. "Why do you have to lock the church?" she said.

"Good question," Father Louis said glancing back at her, "I wish we didn't."

"So why do you?"

They stood at the back by the church entrance. Father Louis studied her for a moment. "I can leave the church open if you'd like to stay a while."

She hesitated. Father Louis looked at her more carefully. "We can talk if you'd like," he said.

"I'd like to ask you something," she said.

"Okay, fine," Father Louis said, ushering her to one of the back pews. "Let's sit here for a while. I have time."

They sat down in the semi-darkness, side by side. The woman reached into her purse and handed the priest a letter envelope. "I would like you to read this," she said.

Father Louis removed the letter and glanced at it. It had obviously been folded and unfolded many times. He held it up to the light behind them.

"It's addressed to Monica," he said. "Is that you?"

She nodded.

"You know," Father Louis said putting the letter down, "it's too dark here. Can't you just tell me what it says?"

"I'd prefer you to read it," she said, sweeping her hair back with a toss of her head. "Isn't there light somewhere?"

Father Louis stood up and led her to the little reconciliation room at the side of the nave where the priests hear confessions. He turned on a soft light and offered the woman the seat across from him. He sat down and looked at the letter. It was handwritten in a bold, agitated script. He could feel the eyes of the woman watching as he read.

Monica,

You don't know me. I am a friend of Margaret Boyer, Charlie Boyer's wife. I am writing this to make sure you know all the grief you have brought upon that poor family. Margaret tried to take her own life three days ago and is in the hospital. First it was Charlie, now it's Margaret, thanks to you. We don't know if she is going to make it. I'm sure you couldn't care less. I am taking care of their son Billy. None of us will ever get over what you have done to this beautiful family.

I hope the truth haunts your sleep for the rest of your life. I can't imagine what kind of woman you are. I pray to God he makes you pay.

The letter was left unsigned.

Father Louis looked up. "Why are you showing me this?" he said.

She made no answer. She lifted up the collar of her coat. "It's cold in here," she said, her eyes never moving from the priest. "Isn't there any heat?"

Father Louis shrugged helplessly. "Who is Charlie?"

"He was my department head," she said. "I worked for him."

"He's dead?"

"He was killed in an automobile accident, two weeks ago," she said looking at him directly, without a sign of emotion.

Father Louis fell silent. He had sat in this confessional across from many different people, people with all kinds of wounds on their consciences. Sometimes they would say *Bless me, Father, for I have sinned* and then they would blurt it out. For others it would take time and patience before they could get to the sticking point.

Father Louis returned her look. He tried to make out what it was he saw in this woman's eyes. It was not something he could name. She was very attractive. A hard kind of beauty, he decided.

He handed the letter back to her. "Are you a Catholic?" he asked.

Monica hesitated. "I suppose I am," she said. "When I was a kid."

"Did you want to make a confession?" he said.

Monica laughed and tossed her head. "Confession," she said, "I haven't been to confession since parochial school."

"That doesn't matter," Father Louis said.

"Look," she said, leaning forward in her chair, "I'm not in the market for sympathy." She brushed her hair back from her face. "What I need right now is some smart advice."

The priest just looked at her quizzically.

"The woman who wrote that letter got me fired," she said. "And she calls me in the middle of the night and just hangs up. I know it's her. She claims Charlie slammed into that overpass intentionally, and she's telling everyone that it's supposed to be my fault somehow."

Father Louis was peering at her now.

"I plan to sue her," she said leaning back. She smoothed her tresses and waited for the priest opposite her to say whatever he had to say.

35

Father Louis sighed. "You want a lawyer," he said. "Why come to a priest?"

"I have a lawyer," she said leaning forward again. "I don't need another lawyer."

"And now you have a priest," Father Louis said managing a smile. "But why?" he asked. "What is it you want?"

The woman bent towards Father Louis, dropping her eyes as she spoke, looking up once or twice to gauge his reaction.

"We were on a business trip to Chicago," she began. "For the company. Charlie and I. He picked me out to go with him, from over ten of us in our department. It wasn't my idea," she said. "He had this *thing* about me. I knew he was married, but he was pretty insistent, you know. He told me it would be good for my career and all that usual . . . bullcrap."

Monica paused and looked straight into the priest's eyes. Perhaps it was the cold that somehow made his eyes seem so distant, so far away. It never occurred to her that he might be praying.

"Anyway," Monica said, straightening up, "when we were in Chicago my boss wanted to get this violin for his son. The kid is crazy about the violin and is taking lessons, or anyway he was. Charlie said the kid had zero ear for a stringed instrument, but the kid loved it, and when we were in Chicago Charlie decided to get him a really good one. Charlie handled the piano pretty well, and they used to play together sometimes. That's what he told me anyway."

Monica hesitated. She drew her cashmere tighter

around her throat. "It's ungodly in here," she complained.

Father Louis said nothing and waited.

Monica shifted in her chair. "This is all so stupid and complicated," she said, half-twisting her body. She drew in a long breath. "You see," she went on, "Charlie was supposed to perform with his kid the day after we were due to get back. At the Suzuki School, for their annual recital or something. I don't know. They were going to play some slow movement together, he and his kid. Charlie said it sounded pretty awful." She thrust the fingers of both hands through her hair and raked it back. She sat straight up and paused to calm her breathing.

"The recital was a big deal for the kid," she began again at length. "To have his daddy there," she said. Another pause. "I guess we didn't realize what it meant to him." Monica shivered and drew her arms around her body.

"I'm sorry it's so cold," Father Louis said. "We don't have the funds to heat an empty church during the week." He moved as if to get up. "We could go into the rectory," he said. "There's hot coffee."

Monica shook her head. "I'll be all right."

Father Louis settled back. A blast of icy wind just then shook the tiny stained glass window behind him. He could feel its chill on the back of his head.

"I take it that recital never came off," he said.

Monica's eyes grew wide. "Yes, that's right."

"And why is that?" he asked. He knew he was not far from the nub.

"Charlie missed the concert," Monica said.

37

"And why was that?" the priest persisted.

"We stayed on in Chicago an extra two days," Monica said.

"Was that because of company business?"

Monica shook her head. "OK," she said, "I have to be honest with you. We stayed on because we were having an affair."

Father Louis remained perfectly still, every muscle of his body at peace. The story was out, this much of it at least. He regarded the young woman across from him, feeling her grow more uncomfortable by the minute. How many times had he seen someone like her before in that chair, perhaps not so stunning, but the story more or less the same. Was the sin so terribly serious? God only knows. But if it was, the lucky ones were filled with remorse. Then there were the hard ones, hoping somehow to turn sin into something that just happened. Beyond these were the legions fighting the fact that sin has its names.

"The boy's name is Billy," Father Louis said. "Is that right?"

"Yes, Billy," Monica said.

"How old was he?"

"He was nine, I think," Monica said.

"When did this happen?" Father Louis asked.

"Three weeks ago."

"And you say the boy's father, this Charlie, may have killed himself crashing into, was it an overpass?" Father Louis said.

Monica made a frown. "He must have been pretty

drunk. He liked his drink."

Father Louis leaned back. The conversation seemed to be going nowhere. "You said you wanted some advice," he said.

Monica nodded and bent toward the priest. "It has to do with the violin," she said. "I told you Charlie got this violin for his kid, when he realized he was going to miss the recital. He called his wife and made up this story about being delayed, and how he wasn't going to be able to make the recital, etc., etc. That didn't go down well with the wife to say the least, and especially with the kid."

"Charlie talked to the kid," she went on, "told him he had a big surprise for him . . . all this with me right there next to him in the hotel room. How do you think I felt?" she said, looking accusingly at the priest. "What was worse," she said with a toss of her hair, "the wife called back to the room right after that and said the kid had just smashed his foot down on his violin. Charlie tried to calm her down. He told her not to worry, he was bringing home a new violin for Billy, a really good one. She told Charlie Billy said he was finished with playing. Charlie told her the kid would get over it and not to worry. He was really sorry, but he had important business that would keep him there in Chicago for a couple of days." Monica let out a bitter laugh at this last recollection.

Monica stood up and wrapped her arms around her body. The wind outside pounded against the room's little window. The chill in the room was becoming unbearable. Father Louis stood up as well and said, "I think we should go next door to the rectory."

Monica shook her head. "No," she said, "I'm almost finished. I just need to know what to do with this violin," she said.

"The violin?"

"Yes, the stupid violin," Monica said. "I have it. Charlie gave it to me to hold until things in his life got straightened. You see, his wife found out he had lied about the delay. I don't know how she found out. Maybe she called the company, or they called her asking about Charlie . . . when he didn't show up for work. He was a big man in the company, and he did what he wanted. That's the way he was. Or maybe somebody from the company saw us together, and that got back to her somehow. I don't know. Anyway, she called him at the hotel the last day and it was pretty traumatic. And I'm right there next to him, having to listen to it all. She was practically screaming. It was definitely not something I needed to hear."

"You still have the violin?" Father Louis said.

"I have the violin," she said. "And I don't know what to do with it." Monica made a brusque gesture. "It's sitting there in my place, and it's like driving me nuts," she said.

"And you're asking me what I think you should do with it? " Father Louis said.

"Please," she pleaded.

Sounds of a slammed door echoed from the sacristy at the other end of the church. Father Louis opened the confessional door and peered out. "That you, Tim?" he called as a figure approached him in the semi-darkness.

Father Tim stepped into the light from the little room. "I was wondering what happened to you," he said, brushing snow from his hair. He glanced inside the little room and saw the woman. "Sorry," he said. He turned to Father Louis. "I need the car keys," he said. "We got a call from the hospital."

"They're on my bureau," Father Louis said.

"No, I looked," Father Tim said.

Father Louis searched his pockets and came up empty. "I'll be over in a sec," he said. "We're just finishing up."

"No great rush," his assistant said. "Traffic accident. Some guy wearing a St. Christopher medal." With that Father Tim retreated back into the half-darkness.

Father Louis turned to Monica and regarded her for a long moment. "Look," he said, "I have no idea what you should do with this violin. Do what you think is best."

Monica moved to leave. "You're a big help," she said.

Father Louis led her to the front doors of the church. "I could help you," he said. "But not about the violin. You're going to have to solve that one yourself."

Monica stood there by the huge twin doors of the entrance, her collar up tight around her throat, bracing for the elements swirling just outside. The priest leaned against one of the heavy doors, fighting the wind to let her out. It was only ten o'clock in the morning but the light of a hard winter day was already failing. Monica turned to the priest, raising her voice to be heard above the wind. "I know what you're thinking," she said.

"I'm sorry I can't do more for you," the priest said, wearily shaking his head. "I really am." The day was miserable enough to begin with.

He pushed the door open and, after a moment of

hesitation, the woman stepped out into icy wind. Then she stopped and spun around to the priest, her hair whipping across her face. Father Louis pulled the door shut as she shouted, "It's not my fault." She stood there for a moment struggling with her hair. Then the lock of the door snapped shut. "It's not my fault," she said, this time to herself as she turned away.

Father Louis went back out through the sacristy and bucked the windy yards to the rectory. He entered the kitchen and found his assistant seated at the table bent over the newspaper, hat and gloves waiting at his side.

"I found the keys," Father Tim said, looking up.

"Where were they?"

"On your desk," Father Tim said. "Sorry about that. Didn't realize you were hearing confession."

Father Louis let out a little laugh. "If you want to call it that," he said pouring himself some coffee. "Talk about anti-matter. What I heard just now was anti-confession."

"We could use some anti-snow right now," Father Tim said, getting up.

Father Louis saw that his young assistant had his boots on. He studied him for a moment. "Have you read the Office for today yet?" he said.

"No."

"The psalm there is for us." Warmth came back into Father Louis's face as he intoned the words from memory:

All you winds, bless the Lord
Cold and chill, bless the Lord
Frost and chill, bless the Lord
Ice and snow, bless the Lord

"Read it," Father Louis said. "Good words for a day like this."

"Yeah, right," the young priest said. He gulped down the remains of his coffee, grabbed his things and went out.

Father Louis listened to the sounds of the garage door struggling up, and the car engine groaning to finally turn over. One of these days they would have to find money to fix the second car. At least find the other set of keys.

The older priest drained his coffee cup and put it in the sink. He went into his office with its big, old, cluttered desk, and right behind it the prie-dieu. The kneeler was old and worn and had been in his family for generations, brought over by great grandparents from the old country. It was given him by his mother and father the day he became a priest. So that he would remember to pray for them, they said. All those years ago.

Father Louis idly leafed through the messages on his desk, glanced absently around the room, and, almost as an afterthought, slowly sank down on the prie-dieu. The whole world was quiet now, buried in the gift of snow and cold, bitter wind. There was nothing else he had to do. Head in hands, he tried not to hear her haunting cry, *It's not my fault, it's not my fault, it's not my fault.* He began to utter barely audible words he had uttered so many times before, and would utter again and again as long as there was life in his priesthood. Did it do any good? It was a question that had always accompanied his prayers like an instrument weaving its steady

43

counterpoint. But that morning, as the priest drifted off into another world, such thoughts would vanish from sight like someone drowning.

Monica

THERE WASN'T A GUY IN THE FIFTH FLOOR Women's Wear buying office, single or married, who wasn't aware of the new hire that first morning as soon as she reported for work. She was that stunning. This great looker was to be Sidney Kramer's latest buying assistant, and Sidney, the company's hot shot women's coat and suit buyer, certainly knew how to find them. As soon as the office guys laid eyes on her, they knew old Sidney'd slammed one over the fence. And the way things always worked with Sidney's finds, before long this one too would get sent out to one of the stores as assistant women's coat and suit manager, and with her looks she'd be off to a smart career. No one foresaw it would be any different this time.

That first morning when the office manager, Marsha Lavain, led this young lady to her desk, the guys were already peering over the cubicle dividers. "This is Monica," she announced to no one in particular. "Sidney's new assistant." Her brusqueness let everyone know she, for one, wasn't buying.

The single guys in the office, though, were sold in an

instant. One by one they found cause to idle past this new hire's cubicle. To say Monica was easy to look at doesn't begin to tell the story.

"Did you see her?" Marty Goldman said rolling his eyes at the others during their ritual, mid-morning coffee break. Marty Goldman was the women's footwear buyer. He was single and had a legitimate interest in such things. It didn't hurt that the new hire's cubicle was just two down from his.

"She's a looker, all right," Stu Harris said. "But tight as a clam." Stu was women's accessories buyer. He was divorced and hungry and had been the first to go in and try chatting her up.

"She married?" Marty asked.

"Don't waste your time," Stu said. "We got ourselves a Greta Garbo. She vants to be alone," he smirked, quoting the famous line from the beautiful but reclusive Swedish actress back in the early days of film.

"I couldn't see a ring," Marty said.

"She's single," Roger Clarkson said. Roger Clarkson was the company's attorney and one of the keenest legal heads in the garment district. He was married and had twin boys he liked to show off at work. Roger's office was on the sixth floor in Legal and he had yet to see this particular new hire. But he had her file opened on his desk.

Sidney Kramer himself joined them at table just then and broke out into one of his feigned lurid grins. He didn't have to guess what they were talking about.

"Listen, you guys," he said, "I knew she was *hot* the moment I laid eyes on her. She's one classy number, and smart too. If she sticks with this rotten business, believe me, she'll go places." And then with the customary gesture he added, "And I'm talkin' *svelte* . . . " Sidney was on his third marriage and seemed to have settled down more or less, but everyone knew old Sidney still had eyes.

Sidney's hamming got a laugh from the table save for the attorney, Roger Clarkson. "And you!" Sidney said turning on him. "What's this about you poking into her background." He said this with that joking scowl you could never be quite sure about.

Roger hunched his shoulders. Sidney was not one of his favorites. "Marsha put her file on my desk," he said evenly. "I'm to look into it."

"Marsha," Sidney scowled with a wave of the hand. "It's all bullcrap, believe me."

Roger looked around at the others, hesitating, then decided Marty and Stu were safe enough. "It seems she lied to get this job," he said. Looking at Sidney he added, "Not very smart, that."

Sidney grabbed his coffee and got up. "Show me an honest bum in this business," he said. With that he moved off to another table.

When Stu left too, Marty leaned over to Roger. "What's going on?" he said. "She lie on her application?"

Roger nodded, adding, "According to Marsha, her last employer fired her. I'm to find out why." Roger said this with another of his shrugs. Far as he was concerned it was just another day at the office.

Marty shook his head. "You know Sidney's gonna fight you."

"Maybe," Roger said looking at his watch and getting up. "We'll see what we find. I'm going to be seeing her this afternoon."

"Some guys have all the luck," Marty said.

The new hire stood in Roger's doorway, waiting for him to look up.

"You wanted to see me," she said in a voice that was soft but hardly short of confidence.

"Ah, yes, . . . Monica. Thanks," Roger said waving her in. The woman was not anything like he expected.

Roger shifted forward motioning her to take a seat. "I thought we should chat," he said, shuffling through some papers on his desk. He glanced up with an awkward smile when he found what he wanted. Then he sank back looking at her without a word. Lawyers will sometimes do that to unsettle a person they're about to interrogate, but that wasn't the case here. The woman slipping into the seat before him was not just another great looker. Roger had seen more than his share in the garment trade. No. It was simply the quiet way she sat there, her presence suddenly transforming the space in his office.

"I have your application," he said, catching himself. Peering down at the document in his hands, he asked too abruptly, "You're thirty?" She looked like she might be a tad older than that.

Monica hesitated. "Isn't that what it says?" she answered not unpleasantly.

48

Roger had to laugh at himself. "Right," he said, "but you know how thirty sometimes can become a round number . . ." It was stupid and he let it go.

"You have an MBA from NYU," he went on, looking up from the document.

"It's pending," she said.

"It doesn't say that here," Roger said.

"It's my thesis," Monica said simply. "My advisor still has it." Then in the next breath she added, "I don't think she has a problem with it." When Roger didn't respond, Monica quickly added, "I've completed all the other requirements."

"I see," Roger said, more himself now. "By the way, what was your topic?"

"Market chaos theory," she said.

"That must have been fun," he said with a chuckle.

"The topic was my advisor's idea," she said, tossing hair back. Then she said, "There's a lot of math. To be honest, I'm not sure I understand the theory."

"I see," Roger said again. He rather liked that.

Settling back, he said, "Tell me a little about your last job."

After a moment, Monica replied coolly, "Well, let's see. I worked there for five years. I started out entry-level in customer support, and then pretty soon they moved me into marketing. It was supposed to be a promotion."

"It didn't turn out that way?" Roger said.

Monica looked down. "I got some nice raises," she said, adding after a pause, "while it lasted."

"They let you go," Roger said, pointing to the application.

"Yes," Monica said.

"Was there some reason?" Roger said.

"I told Miss Lavain the company was cutting back," Monica said, making a fine point.

"You told Marsha Lavain," Roger repeated, waiting.

"That's not the entire story," she said quickly. After a pause, brushing hair away, she leaned forward and said, "I was fired."

Roger smiled and nodded to her. "Yes, that's what we understand." Then he said, "Did the company tell you why?"

Monica didn't answer this. She moved back in her chair.

"There were personal reasons," she said finally.

"I see," Roger said, "but you were a good worker."

"It was quite personal," she said, looking away. "I'd just rather not go into it."

"Monica," Roger said, leaning over his desk, "I have to be candid with you. We can't keep employees who misrepresent themselves. So if there was some circumstance, you know, perhaps some personnel issue, not getting along with your boss, whatever. It would be helpful . . . "

Monica did not answer right away, but she knew this manager, or whoever he was, had shifted to her side. She glanced over at him with a guarded, telling look and said, "Sometimes you can get along too well."

Roger didn't miss the meaning. "Yeah, those things

can happen," he said. "We just needed to clarify that," he added getting up.

"You know, maybe we should have a drink sometime," he said, leading Monica to the door. "I'll give you the rundown about your new boss. He's quite a handful, Sidney."

Without saying anything Monica touched his hand and left. Roger stood in his doorway taking in the lithe, graceful slimness of her form as she moved down the hall. He went back to his desk shaking off what he had seen. And that idea of having a drink sometime, where'd that come from?

Late that afternoon Marty Goldman got Roger on the phone and persuaded him to go down to The Jug after work for a quick one. The Jug was the watering hole off the lobby of their office building. Roger said he should get home but his friend Marty persisted.

"So tell me," Marty said once they had their drinks, "how'd it go?"

"How'd what go?" Roger teased.

"You're not the only one who got to talk to her, you know. I ran into her right after she left you," Marty said.

"Bully for you," Roger said affecting no interest.

"I introduced myself," Marty said. "I didn't jump her," he added with a laugh. "I restrained myself."

Roger made a face. "She's no liar, by the way," he said, wincing down a shot of Stoli. He began looking to get away.

"Sidney'd love that," Marty said. Then he added, "You know, we chatted a bit."

"And?" Roger said, leaning back on the bar. "What'd she say?"

"I offered to show her some of the ropes," he said. "Maybe have lunch sometime. Warn her about old Sidney."

"Sidney," Roger said shaking his head. But interest was there now.

Marty sipped his drink. "Actually," he said with a grin, "I just wanted to let her know what a nice guy I am." He laughed again and swirled the ice in his scotch.

"She take you up on lunch?" Roger asked.

"I wish," Marty said. "She's a bit standoffish. You find her that way?"

Roger shrugged. He put some bills on the bar and stood away. "I've got to go," he said.

"Hey, by the way," Marty said, "she asked about you."

That brought Roger back to the rail. "What'd she say?"

"She wanted to know who you were," Marty said. "She didn't know you were our erstwhile genius corporate attorney."

Roger grinned, "I guess I forgot who I was."

"Yeah," Marty said, "this one can do that to you."

"She say anything else?" Roger asked.

Marty glanced curiously at his friend, then laughed, "I changed the subject fast as I could."

"I'm out of here," Roger said, backing off. "Good luck with her," he said as he moved away.

"You too," Marty shouted after him.

Nothing much more happened between this Greta

Garbo type and Roger, not until the big blow up involving Sidney. This transpired a few months after Monica had slipped like a pro into the routines of the fifth floor buying office. Sidney had been right about her. Mornings she handled small change from the stores, mostly low volume re-orders and pesky returns. Sidney always handled the big stuff. Some mornings Sidney would let her accompany him into the company's tiny show booths where salesmen from downscale vendors would come with their so-so models draped in whatever it was they were hawking. Sidney rarely did any business that way, it being more a courtesy to the trade than an occasion for dealing. Afternoons, Monica went out on her own to vendor showrooms to expedite shipments and generally keep the company's presence alive in the district. She was very good at that. All she had to do was stroll into a showroom and, to a man, the salesmen moved toward her, no matter they were faced all day with good looking, thinly clad models slipping in and out of garments. Monica's ways were always cool and professional, but invariably she got what she came for. Timing, of course, is everything in the fashion business, and at the approach of each season, stores put tremendous pressure on their buying offices to get their orders out ahead of the competition. Expediting those shipments was a big part of an assistant buyer's job. And during the season if a particular item became hot, reorders had to be filled ASAP for store promotions. The competition was doing the same, which is where Monica's adroit ways with salesmen paid off big. "She's dynamite," Sidney liked telling the front office—Marsha Lavain for one.

But then something happened. It started when Sidney had his assistant go to the showroom of Lady Lanford Fashions, a manufacturer of top-of-the-line women's wear. Monica's assignment was to place a single order for a three-piece pantsuit, an unusually smart item designed by the sensational French couturier, André Bresson. The trade was already buzzing about it. The pantsuit was in soft cassimere twill and was bound to be a mover in the upscale market the coming season.

Sidney naturally got wind of it and wanted to see the item for himself. Problem was he couldn't show his face at Lady Lanford. For one, Lady Lanford clothes were too upscale for his stores, and the salesmen at Lady Lanford Fashions certainly knew it. But basically it was Sidney himself. He was known as a knock-off artist. There'd be no point in his going there.

"Tell them the pantsuit is for you, personally," Sidney said to his assistant. "We'll refund you. And this is important. Get them to promise one off their first run. Maybe they'll let you take one of the floor models." He grinned at Monica, "You're good with salesmen."

What Sidney had in mind of course was just that, a knock-off. He pulled two or three of these high fashion knock-offs every season. It didn't make him popular in the industry, but the company stores loved him—high fashion at everyday prices. Sidney kept a shoe-string loft in the garment district busy with these rip-offs, and he had already lined up a downscale fabric house to supply the cashmette. This imitation cashmere would cut the fabric cost alone by more than half.

The salesmen at Lady Lanford had never seen her before, and the moment Monica walked into the showroom, two of them approached with bright-eyed grins. Their looks faded fast when Monica told them where she was from, and when she mentioned she'd come to see the Bresson pantsuit for herself personally, the two looked at each other. Showrooms of course do not do retail, but they generally accommodate people in the trade, up to a point.

"Sidney put you up to this?" the senior of the two said.

"I said it's for me," Monica said casually, glancing around the showroom. "You have such nice things," she said. "I still have one of your cocktail dresses."

It's just possible that might have been true. In any event, it gave them something to think about besides Sidney.

"Could I try it on at least?" she asked. "I'm a six."

The more senior one shrugged his shoulders and gestured for the other to show her to the dressing room. After a few minutes she reappeared in the Bresson.

"That looks really good on you, honey," one of the models said coming over to her. Several others came out and stood around nodding approval. A buyer at the far end of the showroom walked over, thinking Monica was a model. "Hey, that rocks," he said.

The two salesmen could see for themselves.

Monica went before a full-length mirror, viewing herself at different angles. "It's really lovely," she said to them, adding with a smile. "I'll take it."

The senior salesman threw his head back and laughed. He had to like her moxie.

"I'll wear it out of here," she teased.

"You couldn't afford it," he said, by this time thinking it'd be smart to hire her. He had a huge smile on his face.

"Okay," Monica said playfully, "but promise me a six in black, off the first run."

There was a pause about that, and then the older salesman laughed again and shook his head. "I shouldn't, you know," he said. "Can you swear this won't wind up in Kramer's hands?"

Monica smiled. "I told you it's for me," she said. Sidney Kramer would be proud of her.

The salesmen said, "If you say so. Let's hope you're honest."

"When can I have it?" Monica said after she came back out in her own things, looking virtually as smart.

"We have your word on this, correct?" he said.

Monica smiled. "Would I lie?"

"If you are, you'll hear from us." He said that with a hard laugh.

Monica gave him one of her super smiles and left.

She had done Sidney's dirty work, but now on the way back to the office the salesman's parting remark stuck. When Monica related her misgivings to Sidney, he dismissed it with a wave. "Naw," he said. "Listen, there's no copyright on this stuff. You've got nothing to worry about." Normally, at a time like this in the past, Sidney would drape a reassuring arm about the understudy, but here he was dealing with their own Greta Garbo. "Listen, sweetheart," he said, "forget about this. Copycatting is the name of fashion."

Monica took Sidney at his word. If anybody knew this business it was certainly him. But when she went back to Lady Lanford Fashions a week later to pick up the pantsuit, the salesman she had charmed appeared all business now. He handed her the garment bag with a curt, "This better not be going to Sidney Kramer." It was clear he meant it.

All Monica could answer was, "I said it's for me."

Monica handed Sidney the garment bag and told him she was really worried now. He brushed it off, telling her she did great. She should just forget about Lady Lanford. "They can't do a thing," he said.

Monica wasn't satisfied with that and went up to the sixth floor to see Roger. He was a lawyer. He would know if she'd gotten herself into something.

"I need to talk to you," she mouthed when Roger looked up at her in his office doorway. He was on the phone.

Roger put his hand over the receiver and said, "I can't now." He pointed to his watch and held up a single finger. "One hour, okay?"

Monica had not been back at her desk ten minutes when her phone rang. It was Roger.

"I'm sorry," he said, "I'm going to be tied up all afternoon. Is it something important?"

"I think so."

"OK, look, meet me down at The Jug right after work. Five-thirty. We can talk then."

And that's what they did. Monica told him about the pantsuit affair and the verbal assurance the Lady Lanford salesman had wrought from her. Roger listened dutifully, asked a few questions, and said he didn't think it was anything to worry about. Sidney was right. These knock-offs are par for the course in this business.

"But I agreed to something that wasn't true," Monica said.

"Yeah, Sidney put you on the spot," Roger said. "But he's right. What can they do?"

Monica seemed satisfied and they didn't stay long, not even for drinks.

Sidney had wasted no time getting the knock-off under way, and before long, not too surprisingly, scuttlebutt about it reached Lady Lanford Fashions. What Lady Lanford did next was swift and virtually unheard of in the district. They filed a law suit against the company seeking a court injunction against the company's action, asserting breach of verbal agreement as the basis of the complaint, with the usual claim to plaintiff's potential pecuniary damages. The company, Sidney, and Monica were all three cited as defendants. Subpoenas to that effect were served on each of the defendants late one afternoon.

As soon as she was served, Marsha Lavain had Roger come to her office. She handed him the subpoena.

Roger glanced through the pages. Looking up, he said, "It's nothing serious. They're hitting on Sidney."

"It says here that she misrepresented the company," she said frowning. "This Monica lied to them."

"She's not a liar," Roger said, "take my word for it."

"I wonder," Marsha said. "Anyway, you'll look into it. We can't have this."

In the next instant, Sidney burst into her office, the subpoena in his hand. "They sure hate my guts," he said flopping down in a seat.

"You might have left the poor girl out of your games," Roger said to him.

Sidney laughed. "Oh, come on," he said. "It's good for her. Toughen her up." Turning to Marsha, Sidney winked, "I notice no one minds my games at bonus time."

That got a smile from Marsha. Whatever she felt about Sidney, he did make money for them.

She looked over at Roger. "What do we tell the sixth floor?" she asked, referring to the company's executive suite down the hall from Roger.

"I'll put some depositions together," he said. "We'll deny the whole thing."

Marsha nodded. Turning to Sidney, she said, "Monica went to Lady Lanford on her own, right?"

"Absolutely," Sidney said.

Marsha looked back at Roger. "You'll work this story out with her," she said. Then she added, seemingly apropos of nothing, "I saw you with her at The Jug the other evening."

"I had to calm her down," he said. "This thing has gotten to her."

"I'll bet," Marsha said dryly.

Marsha and Sidney put their heads together about an unrelated matter. Roger reached for the subpoena and got up to leave. As he stepped away, Marsha called out pointedly, "Roger, you don't bring the twins anymore. We haven't seen them for months."

Roger had no ready answer for that. He went straight to Monica's cubicle and found her sunk back in her chair, pale white, the subpoena in her lap.

"Let's go down for a drink," he said quietly. "We can't talk here."

"It's not serious," Roger assured her as soon as they settled at the back of The Jug and ordered drinks. "There was no binding agreement."

"But there was," Monica said.

"No," Roger said. "You're an employee, not a legal company rep. Your word meant nothing. And they know that. They're just trying to take Sidney down a peg or two."

"And me, too," Monica said.

"Yes, unfortunately, but it means nothing," he said.

"So what will happen?" Monica said after a silence.

"I don't see anything happening," Roger said. "It'll keep us lawyers busy for a while, that's all."

The drinks came and Roger lifted his glass. "Here's to better days," he said.

"I guess I ought to drink to that," Monica said, a hint of color returning to her face.

Roger leaned forward and touched her hand. "I'm sorry this has happened," he said. "You didn't deserve this."

Monica didn't move her hand right away. "I should have known better," she said making an effort to return his smile.

Roger finished his drink. "Care for another?" he said.

"If you like," she said, still nursing the one she had.

Roger came back with the drinks and this time he plunked himself down right next to her.

"Look, Monica," he said, "I know this is tough on you. But, I have to be honest, I'm not entirely sorry this happened. It's giving me a chance to know you better."

Roger laughed at himself and tossed down his second shot of *Stoli*.

Monica brushed a hand across his. "I do appreciate the help," she said. "Honestly."

"My pleasure," Roger said, signaling to the waiter. He ordered another drink for himself. Monica was still one behind.

For a while neither spoke. Finally Monica glanced at the man who had seated himself a bit too close. "Marsha told me you have twins," she said, "twin boys."

"They're great kids," Roger said looking away. Then, after a silence, he turned and looked straight at her. "Monica, I have to share something with you, about me," he said. Roger swallowed his drink and began to talk about his marriage, never naming his wife, how at first he had such great expectations, about the big hole that gradually developed. "I kept hoping for something that just wasn't there," he said, his voice almost choking.

"I'm terribly sorry," Monica said softly.

"Yeah, me too," Roger said, half embarrassed with himself. He pushed Monica's drink towards her. "Monica, drink up," he said. "Maybe we'd better call it a day."

Monica didn't stir but just kept regarding him. "Thank

you for telling me that," she said. "It makes you seem more . . . " she hesitated and did not finish the sentence.

"More what?" Roger said brightening a little.

"I don't know," Monica said laughing now. "Maybe more . . . knowable."

That got Roger. He leaned closer to Monica and said, almost blushing, "I'm terribly glad you wanted, you know, to figure me out." He laughed. "I've been trying to do that all my life."

The waiter came by just then and Roger signaled for another round but Monica delicately waved him off. "Not now," she said to Roger. "Some other time, okay?"

Outside, as they parted, Roger's head was spinning.

Monica waved down a cab. "Shouldn't you be taking a cab?" she said, regarding him.

"Not a problem," Roger said merrily. "I'm sober as a judge."

Monica actually let him kiss her.

As he drove home, happy as a kid, Roger suddenly realized he had forgotten to set up Monica for the deposition, for the story he had to persuade her to tell. The thought of it focused him like a splash of ice water.

First thing the next morning Roger had Monica come to his office.

"I really like the way it went last night," he said rising to his feet when she entered.

"I see you made it home in one piece," she said in a smile that for her was almost warm.

"Yes, well," Roger hesitated. He wanted more than anything to pick up the threads of the previous evening, but this unpleasantness had to be gotten out of the way. His boss gave him 'til noon.

"Monica," he said, "you know what a deposition is, don't you?"

"I guess I *do*," she said more or less playfully. "And I imagine you want one from me, right?"

"You're way ahead of me," he said.

"And if I'm not mistaken," she went on, "it's taken under oath, right? The whole truth and nothing but the truth?"

Roger left that alone. "Sidney, you know, has to be deposed too. All three defendants do," he said.

Monica looked hard at him. She hadn't thought about Sidney.

Roger ploughed on. "I'm sure you appreciate the stories have to match," he said. "Yours and Sidney's."

"Is that a problem?" Monica asked, aware suddenly that it very well would be.

"It is if the stories don't agree," he said.

Monica grew silent. Roger waited for the inevitable question, but Monica wasn't going to make it easy for him.

Finally, he said uncomfortably, "Sidney's story has to be that he had nothing to do with your going to Lady Lanford. Nor did anyone else in the company."

Monica sank back in her chair. "He's asking me to lie," she said, speaking to the walls as much as to Roger. Looking back squarely at him she declared, "You're really asking me to perjure myself."

"We don't have a choice," Roger said, palms rising in defense. "For the good of the company," he added.

"For the good of the company," Monica repeated. She looked around in mock disbelief.

"Monica, we have to do this," he went on lamely. "The company can't be dragged into it. It has its reputation to consider."

"And mine?" Monica said.

"You'll be all right," Roger said. "You told that salesman one thing, you did another. So what? What can they do? What law did you break?"

Monica just stared at him and said nothing.

"Look," Roger said, leaning forward, "It's not complicated. All you have to say is that you went to Lady Lanford Fashions on your own nickel. No one from the company put you up to anything. It was your idea to show the stupid pantsuit to Sidney. He liked it and asked you for it. I'll ask you why you thought he wanted it, and you can tell the truth. And that's it. That's your deposition."

"And Sidney will be free," Monica came back sarcastically. "As he says, stealing is the name of fashion."

"Anyway, it's not illegal," Roger said.

"So I'm the only one who's done anything wrong," Monica said, standing up. "I lied to them, but it doesn't matter."

Roger got up too. "Monica, we have no choice," he said. "We have to do this, today."

She turned to him at the door. "At least let me think about it," she said.

He went up to her, putting his hand on a slender shoulder. "I don't like this any more than you," he said. "We really don't have a choice."

After a pause, Monica felt for his hand and said, "I suppose you're right."

Early that afternoon, Roger led her down the hall to an executive conference room where a court reporter was set up and waiting. Sidney was already there, along with the company's vice president for public affairs, Roger's superior. He was to be the company's defendant. Roger wasted no time. He had them each in turn raise their right hand and repeat the formulaic words about the truth, then he deposed them, the VP first, Sidney next, and then Monica. Everything transpired just as expected, with all the denials called for in the expected places. When it was over, the vice president grabbed Sidney and took off, barely nodding to Roger. Monica he ignored entirely, though truthfully, throughout the session his glance kept sliding over to this recent employee of theirs, the cause of all this bother. You can be sure Monica was not unaware of these looks. No supremely attractive woman ever is, like it or not.

Roger settled some matters with the court reporter, and then the two of them were alone. Gathering up papers, he looked over at Monica. "Well, all right!" he sighed merrily. "We got through that one. From now on it's all downhill. The plaintiff will take their depositions too, but this will never make it to trial, believe me." Roger placed an arm on her shoulder. "You did great, by the way."

Monica said nothing. As they went back towards his office, Roger suggested they meet after work, at The Jug, in the usual spot at the back.

"We can both use a stiff one," he laughed.

"We need something," Monica said, almost to herself.

Then it was back to work for them both.

After work, Roger got to their watering hole first, to their usual spot in the back. Some minutes later Monica came along and slid in across from him.

"Everything okay?" Roger said, reaching for her hand but not finding it.

"Sure," Monica said with barely a smile, brushing back her hair.

They ordered drinks and sat there, looking around, saying little, skirting the inevitable topic. Then after a silence, Monica asked him, "Do you believe in hell? That there is such a place?"

Roger did a double take. "That's an odd question," he said. "What brought that on?"

"I know," she said with a faint smile. "But do you?"

Roger shook his head. "Well, let's say I believe there's hell on earth," he said. "For some people."

Monica looked away and fell silent again.

Roger reached and took her hand. "Is this nonsense still eating you?" he said.

She shook her head and withdrew the hand for her drink. "I was just wondering," she said, "what you thought about such things . . . "

Roger had to laugh. "I'm a Catholic, you know," he said. "More or less. I guess to be honest you'd have to say less," he added with a laugh.

"You Catholic by any chance?" he said, peering at her.

"I used to be," she said, trying to smile.

"We have that in common, too," he said. "I'm glad."

They sat there for a while sipping their drinks, glancing around, glancing back at each other, he more than she, saying little.

Then, with a hopeful smile, Roger slid his hand over hers.

"Where are we going with this?" she said looking down at what he had done.

Roger didn't answer right away. The flatness in her voice hurt, and he drew his hand away. A couple being seated just then at a table nearby allowed him to look away. Then, turning back he said, "Monica, have you ever noticed you never speak my name. Not once."

Monica smiled. "I know," she said.

"Why?" he asked.

At first she didn't answer. "It's funny about names," she said at length with a faint smile. "They're sort of like glue sometimes. Like they have a way of sticking to you."

Roger leaned over and took hold of both her hands. "I keep hoping something might happen," he said. "You know, between us. Something real."

"That might be nice," she said, concealing the effort.

Just then some others from the company came into The Jug and made their way to the bar. Roger saw Marty and Stu among them. Monica turned and saw them too.

"Tonight's not our night," he said. "They've already spotted us." Leaning close to Monica he said, "Let's do this again tomorrow, okay? It's Saturday, and we can have the whole afternoon."

"But what about your family?"

"It'll be all right," he said. "I often come in on Saturdays."

He got up and extended a hand. "Maybe we can, you know, talk things over."

Monica got up on her own and said nothing.

As they approached the others at the bar, Marty raised his drink to Monica. "Well, well, well," he said. "Look what we have here—party of the second part huddled with her erstwhile mouthpiece." He puckered his lips.

"I don't call that funny," Roger said evenly.

"Hey, I thought you said this case was a joke," Marty laughed. "Nothing to it, right?"

Stu placed his hand on Monica's back. "Don't worry your pretty head over any of this," he said. "Sidney just laughs about it."

Marty signaled to the bartender and leaned close to Monica. "What are you having?"

Monica shook her head. She turned to Roger. "I'm sorry," she said. "I really have to go."

"I'll take you," Roger said, "I'm leaving too."

"It isn't necessary," Monica said. "I'll grab a cab."

Monica turned to the others with a fleeting smile and walked away, not saying a word. Roger caught up as she stepped outside.

"Is anything wrong?" he asked.

"It's been a long day," she said. "I'm terribly tired."

"Let me take you," he said.

"You stay with your friends," she said waving down a cab.

"Is your place far?" Roger asked, opening the cab door for her. He had no idea where she lived.

"Not really," she said as she slipped in.

"Two o'clock tomorrow, okay?" he called. "In our booth at the back." She looked up and smiled in what he took for assent.

He went back to Marty and Stu at the bar but none of them stayed very long.

Roger was at The Jug early that Saturday afternoon, well ahead of time. He was dressed in Saturday casuals and felt relaxed and pleased with himself. Monica would be along in a while. They'd have a few drinks, talk, then in the best of all worlds they would go to her place. She was single and lived nearby, far as he knew.

He sat there in their usual booth near the back of the bar. The place was empty on a Saturday, just he and the barkeep. On signal, the bartender came over and Roger ordered another drink. By now Monica was late, but he didn't mind having time to mull things over. So much had happened so fast, so unexpectedly. It's true he barely knew her, and yet he had no doubt she was what had always been missing. She had it all, everything he ever wanted—all you could hope for on the physical side, and most importantly for him, a quick mind that caught on to your thoughts almost before you had them yourself. But it was just Monica herself that got to him, the lovely, silent, elusive Monica, a woman not like anyone he had ever known but always dreamed might exist somewhere, just for him, a quiet, lovely presence that would complete him if ever she was his. All it would take from her was a certain look, a certain touch.

It hurt some when he thought about his wife, his boys especially, but that could all get worked out somehow, like it always has for half the world. He needed something now for himself.

Roger looked at his watch. It was well after two. She was more than late. He went up and sat at the bar. He half-watched a dull ballgame on a huge overhead screen, keeping an eye on the door.

By now it was almost three. He had misread the signs. She never intended . . .

Roger felt stupid, threw some bills on the counter and went up to his office. The sixth floor was dark and empty and going there seemed pointless, but it lessened the untruth to his family. He sat at his desk and glanced idly through some papers. For a long time he just looked at the wall.

On the way home he called and suggested he could bring home a pizza. His wife said she had supper on the stove already.

Midmorning Monday Roger saw his friend Marty suddenly standing there in the doorway of his sixth floor office.

"She's gone!" he announced.

"What do you mean, gone?" Roger said.

"She hasn't shown up," he said shaking his head. "She didn't call in. When Sidney tried getting her, the line was dead. It's been disconnected. She's left us."

70

"I'm not surprised," Roger said evenly with a shrug. "I figured as much."

Marty looked at his friend and left shaking his head with a funny laugh. Moments later Roger went down to Marsha Lavain who confirmed everything. "We won't miss her," she said eyeing Roger. His face struck her as different somehow.

"What about Sidney?" Roger said. He could think of nothing else to say.

"Sidney takes these things in his stride," she said. "It's all the same to him."

"Guess you're right," Roger said. "That's the way the wheel turns." And with that he left.

"Bring the twins around," Marsha called after him. "We miss them."

Roger cleared his desk and brought himself to leave work early that day. He bought some treats for the twins and drove straight to his home.

THE MYSTERIOUS WORKINGS
OF CHRIST'S LOVE
(ELEVEN EPISODES)

1

FATHER LOUIS ENTERED THE RECTORY KITCHEN of St. Andrew's chuckling to himself. He had just come in from saying the Saturday five o'clock Mass. His vicar, Father Tim, slouched with coffee at the kitchen table, looked up with half a smile.

"What's so funny?" he asked.

His superior tossed a business card on the table. "I thought this fellow wanted me to hear his confession," he said. "We go into the reconciliation room, and instead he hands me his business card. Just struck my funny bone I guess."

Father Tim picked up the card. "Ronny's Roofing," he read aloud and laughed. "More power to him," he said turning back to his coffee.

Father Louis poured his own cup. "He probably needs work," he said. "You might look him up while I'm away. Heaven knows our roof's overdue."

"Yeah, with what funds?" the young priest said.

"Good point," Father Louis said with that affable shrug of his.

This brief exchange was followed by the not unfamiliar lapse that often fell between them.

"Who's the chef tonight? I forget," Father Louis said after a while. He had gone over to the fridge to inspect what the housekeeper may have left for a Saturday night.

"Me," Father Tim said, "And I've ordered out." The young priest rose and put two dinner plates on the table. "We can't have leftovers for your last meal."

"My last meal!" Father Louis laughed, moving to help out with the knives and forks.

"You'll do better in Rome, for sure." Father Tim said. "But watch yourself. Don't try to keep up with our bishop, for heaven's sake."

The table was set and they sat down, followed by another break in small talk. Finally Father Louis said, "Tim, I need to speak to you about this priest who's coming to fill in for me, Felix Cooper."

"I do, too," the young priest said. "This guy could be a problem for us."

"How so?" Father Louis said, breaking into a smile.

"I'm serious, Lou," the young priest went on. "There's already some talk about him. I can't believe the bishop would lay this on us."

Father Louis made a wry face. "What are they saying?"

"You can guess what they're saying. You know the woman he was involved with was confirmed in this parish. They still remember her."

"Tim, that's all in the distant past now," the older priest said. "And anyway, Felix has more than paid his dues. Besides, you know I'll be away for two months, at the very least. You'll need the help."

"But why this guy, why Felix Cooper?"

"Who else is there?" Father Louis said. "Anyway, Tim, the bishop feels okay about him now. And I think he might be right about that."

"I heard he wears a pectoral cross," the younger priest said with a jerk of his head. "Like a bishop. I'm surprised the Chancery hasn't called him on it."

Father Louis smiled. "It's a plain wooden cross, without the corpus," he said. "Felix got the bishop's permission. He told the bishop he would be the corpus."

"That's real cute."

His superior looked down and let it drop.

The rectory's front doorbell rang. As the young priest got up, he said over his shoulder, "There's talk in the parish about him, you know."

Father Louis let this pass also.

The young assistant came back into the kitchen with their supper, Sicilian *sacciata*, a favorite of his. He had a beer, Father Louis contenting himself with more coffee.

In the middle of eating, the older priest said, "I see your friend is back."

"I've got a friend?" the young assistant said with one of his ready half-laughs.

"That woman with the Polish surname."

"Oh, yeah," Fr. Tim said, "Monica."

"She was at Mass today," Father Louis said.

"She speak to you?"

"I think she was expecting *you* actually," Father Louis said with a little laugh.

"I've been trying to help her," Father Tim said finishing off his beer. He went to the fridge for another.

"You getting friendly with her?" Father Louis asked after his assistant settled back.

"Friendly?"

"There's been some gossip, you know," Father Louis said.

"To hell with gossip."

"Anyway," Father Louis said off-handedly, "not to repeat it, but you ought to know you were seen with her in a bar and grill, downtown." Then he added, eyebrows raised a hair, "Without your clerics."

"Who told you that?" Father Tim asked making a face.

"Martha says her son, Paul, saw you," Father Louis replied with that easy shrug of his.

"That figures," Father Tim said wryly. "Look," he said leaning forward, "Monica's got her problems. You know that yourself. I'm trying to be a friendly ear."

"I can see she's got problems," Father Louis said. "Just be careful," he said.

"What's that supposed to mean?" Father Tim said putting his food down.

"I don't mean anything by it, Tim," his pastor said. "I don't want this Monica to become your problem, that's all."

"Look," the younger priest said, "she showed up again out of the blue, two weeks ago, right? She wanted to talk and didn't seem comfortable here. You probably don't know this, but she tried to take her life. She's just getting back on her feet."

The older priest nodded at this. "I see that," he said, looking at his assistant with a reassuring smile.

Father Tim stood up and took their plates to the sink.

"By the way," Father Louis said, "I got a call from the bishop, just before Mass. The date's been moved up. We're leaving Tuesday."

"Tuesday!" Father Tim said, swinging around to his superior. "But you won't be here for Felix. You know I've never met this guy. I don't even know what he looks like."

"Don't worry, Tim" the old priest grinned, getting up. "He'll go easy on you."

2

The day after the pastor left for Rome, the young parochial vicar was going through the morning's mail when he heard an argument developing outside his office just off the kitchen. He stepped out to find Martha, the housekeeper, pleading with her son, Paul. They both turned and fell silent when they saw him.

"We're sorry, Father," Martha said. "Paul is being difficult."

"Nothing new in that now, is there," Father Tim said with his half laugh.

"I figure it wasn't your idea, right Father?" Paul said, stepping toward him. "About this defrocked priest coming here."

"He's not an ex-priest, if you're talking about Father Felix," Father Tim said over his shoulder, turning back to his office.

"I know, but he should be."

A bit later, as Father Tim was going out, Martha apologized for her son. "He's so strict," she said.

"Yeah," Father Tim said, "pretty amazing with him studying at Georgetown."

"Father," Martha said, "will you be taking Father Lou's office while he's away? I was wondering where we should place Father Felix."

Father Tim thought about it for a moment. "Let him have Lou's office. He won't be here that long."

3

The next morning, after concluding the nine o'clock Mass, Father Tim was about to shut off the lights and secure the church when he spotted Monica in the last pew. She was alone with her head down, unaware of his approach.

"Hi, there," Father Tim said coming up with a lively step.

Monica, startled for a second, replied, "Oh, hello, Father."

The priest slid into the seat next to her. "You doing okay?" he said.

"I'm all right, Father," she said softly.

"I've been worried about you, you know, since we talked."

Monica said nothing but sort of smiled at the priest who had dumped himself down beside her. She felt his gaze on her and almost imperceptibly shifted in her seat.

"I thought maybe you'd like some coffee or some-thing," he said springing back up. "Our housekeeper's always got something good waiting for us after Mass." He said this as offhandedly as he knew how.

Monica hesitated for an instant then replied, "Sure, Father."

In the rectory, Father Tim introduced Monica to the housekeeper who set about serving them. Then Martha excused herself.

"Father Louis has left?" Monica said, glancing around uneasily.

"Yeah, off to Rome," the young priest said. "They got him on some commission about parish life." Then he added with a laugh, "Maybe it's about parish life-support, whatever."

Monica leaned back a little. "I've never been in a rec-tory before," she said.

"Well, for sure it isn't hallowed ground," Father Tim joked. "Priests have to live too, you know."

"I'm sorry, Father," Monica said. "You have to excuse me. I've been away from all this for so long."

"But you're back, that's what counts," Father Tim said.

Monica laughed to herself, "I'm not sure I am."

"Well, you're here now, anyway."

Monica glanced at the priest. "Father, can I ask you something? I know this might seem a strange question, but I was wondering, you know, about what you believe."

"Believe about what?"

"About everything, Father," she said. "You know, about all these so-called truths of religion. I've been meaning to ask you."

"That is an odd question to ask a priest," he said half laughing.

"I know," she said trying to smile, "But I was just wondering. Priests don't always agree about everything, do they?"

"I believe what the Catholic Church believes and teaches," he said more seriously. "I'm its priest after all."

Monica looked pointedly at the priest and said, "Do you believe in hell?"

The young priest, taken back, reflected for a moment then said, "Well, yes, of course. I'm more or less obliged to. I don't have to believe there's anyone there, though."

"No one hardly talks about it anymore, do they?" Monica said.

"For good reason," Father Tim said with an easy laugh. "People are already scared enough of God."

When Monica didn't react, Father Tim asked, "I hope you're not worried about things like that."

"I don't know, Father," she said. Then she said, "I'm sorry. It's not very pleasant."

"Yeah," Father Tim said. "Amen to that." Refilling her coffee, the young priest picked up on the topic anyway. "The Gospel is about good things, the good news. You understand that, right?"

"You know, Father," she said, shaking her head ever

so faintly, "I've been listening to homilies for a while now. In other parishes, too. I have to tell you that what the priests say doesn't seem to get at what really bothers people, deep down. I'm sorry, but that's the way it comes across."

"Ouch," said Father Tim with a mock toss of the head. "That hurts."

"Really, Father," she went on, "I think in a lot of people there's an ache deep down, like a terribly tender sore spot that never goes away. Just to be told over and over that God loves us; that's all very nice, but it doesn't ever seem to get at that hurt. It's almost as if priests don't know it's there. I never hear them talk about it, anyway."

"Monica, is there any hurt that love can't heal?"

"I suppose you're right, Father," she said, eyes drifting away.

She glanced at her watch. "I'm sorry," she said looking up at him. "I really have to go." She got up. "I do appreciate talking to you," she added. "Maybe we can do this again sometime?"

"Absolutely," Father Tim said, "Anytime. I'll have some free time after the nine o'clock tomorrow, if that works for you."

"I'll probably be at Mass," she said lightly, "though I'm not sure I know why, exactly."

Father Tim escorted her to the door. Opening it for her, he said, "I'm very glad we're talking."

Monica answered with a genuine smile that lit up the loveliest eyes. "I am too, Father," she said.

The young priest hesitated shutting the door. He

watched her as she passed down the walk, then abruptly caught himself and went to his office. Moments later, Martha stuck her head in. "I didn't realize we'd have a guest, Father," she said. "Was there enough of every-thing?"

"Everything was perfect!" he said. Martha noted the assistant pastor had never smiled at her like that before.

4

Mid-afternoon a day later, Father Tim was reading his Office and jotting down some thoughts when Martha popped her head in and announced, "Father Felix is here."

Father Tim dropped everything and went out to the foyer where he found an older priest standing amid a few thin pieces of luggage. Felix Cooper struck him as worn to the point of frailty, even sickliness, not anything like he'd expected. He was in his clerics, unusual anymore for priests traveling. And then there was the good-size wooden cross, hanging down conspicuously to the midsection of Felix Cooper's sunken, priestly chest.

"Felix," Father Tim said stretching out his hand, "I'm Tim. Welcome to St. Andrew's."

"Glad to be here, Tim," Father Felix said. "I was hoping you'd be in." Then, pointing to the two thin bags at his feet, he joked a bit awkwardly, "This is all of me."

"Here, let me help you," Father Tim said, picking them up. "I'm so sorry Lou wasn't here, you know, to welcome you," he said, leading the priest to the spare bedroom in the back.

"Yes," Father Felix said simply. "We were in seminary together."

"Look," the younger priest said, setting the luggage down in the spare room, "why don't you just make yourself at home, then come out to the kitchen. We can have some coffee. Have you had lunch?" he asked.

"Not really."

"I'll have Martha fix you up something, okay?"

"Sounds wonderful," Father Felix said.

When Father Tim went to the kitchen, he found Martha's son, Paul, standing there with his mother.

"I'm surprised to see *you* here," Father Tim said with an effort to be civil.

Martha chimed in, "Paul's taking me to the dentist."

"I'm curious about this priest," Paul said. "He just got here, right?"

Just then Father Felix entered the kitchen. "Hello," he said looking around. "I'm Father Felix. In case you haven't already figured that out," he added with a good laugh. "And you're Martha," he said half bowing to the housekeeper.

"Father, this is my son, Paul," Martha said. "He's getting his PhD at Georgetown. He's home on break now."

"How about that," Father Felix said, reaching out his hand. "What's your field?"

"Philosophy."

"Analytic? Continental?" Father Felix asked.

"Neo-scholasticism," Paul said, pleased with the question.

"Oh, wow," Father Felix said.

He turned to Father Tim. "You must have some interesting conversations."

Father Tim glanced at Martha with an unmistakable look.

"Paul, we should go now," she said.

"Right," Paul said. "But I wanted to ask Father Felix something—about this cross he wears."

Father Tim moved to break this up when the older priest held up his hand. "No, wait," he said. "Let me see if I can satisfy our young friend here." Turning to him, he said, "You ask why the cross?"

He took the wooden cross up in his hand. "I wear this as a sign," he said. "As a Thomist, you know what it signifies."

"I guess I do," Paul said with some amusement.

"I'm sure you do," Father Felix said with an affable nod. "So you know about forgiveness and what it is we're forgiven for, right?"

"Perfidy," Paul said with a caustic edge.

"Right," Father Felix said, breaking out into an easy laugh, "and that's why I have this cross. And why it's so big."

Paul regarded the priest with an ironic squint. "Can't argue with that," he said. Then, with a quick glance at Father Tim, the young philosopher took his mother and departed.

"I'm really sorry," Father Tim said to the older priest after they left. "Not a pleasant guy."

"I rather liked him," Father Felix said.

Father Tim shook his head with a smirk. "He's one of these throwbacks, you know, thinks the world is going to hell in a hand basket."

"Well, he could be right about that, no?"

"Sure, but somebody ought to tell him sin isn't the last word. Love, grace, forgiveness is."

"Can't have forgiveness without the sin, though, right?" Father Felix said lightly.

"Right," Father Tim allowed, "but what did the Apostle say? *Where there's sin, there grace abounds.*"

"I couldn't agree with you more," Father Felix said more quietly, surprised at the direction the conversation had taken. "Grace is everything," he added.

Father Tim got up and looked in the fridge. "I can fix you an egg," he said.

"I'm good," Father Felix said. "Maybe just a slice of bread. I usually skip lunch."

They sat in silence as Father Felix pensively smeared his slice with a thin layer of peanut butter.

After a few moments of this, Father Felix looked over at the young priest who was to be his boss for the next few months. "You mentioned love," he said. "Remember Christ's words in the Gospel? *He who is forgiven much loves much.* I think that's how it works, don't you?" he said, biting into his sandwich.

"That's not how the passage goes, actually," Father Tim said gently. "In *Luke*, as I recall, the love comes first. The sinner is forgiven much because she loved much."

"I know," the old priest said chewing, "But there's the

84

other side to that coin. What did Christ say next? *He who is forgiven little loves little,* right? That to me is the bottom line."

Father Tim let it go.

After more moments of silence, the older priest put his sandwich down. "You know, Tim," he began, "if you don't mind my going on this way, it's a mysterious thing about sin, now that you mention it. Especially serious sin. We know that moral lapses, if they're serious, separate us from God, true enough. But there's this other thing, too. A serious sin can have just the opposite effect. What'd the Psalmist say, *Out of the depths I cry unto thee.* Falls can be like that. They have a way of bringing us back, humbled and empty-handed, like the Prodigal Son." Father Felix had to chuckle as he added, "That's the way Our Lord likes us, isn't it? Humbled and empty-handed."

When Father Tim failed to respond, the old priest said, "Don't you think that's so?"

"Yeah, sure. I guess things can work out that way," the young priest said, fighting a growing unease at this priest's take on things. Felix Cooper seemed to wear this notorious moral lapse of his like a badge.

5

The following morning Father Tim celebrated the nine o'clock, but Monica was not to be seen. Returning to the rectory afterwards, he found Father Felix at the kitchen table. The older priest had celebrated the early Mass and was still nursing after-breakfast coffee. The two greeted each other as a busy Martha put a plate of luscious ham and eggs before the acting pastor. She inquired of Father Felix if he needed anything, commenting that he'd hardly touched his breakfast. He waved her off with a comic gesture and she left them.

"One could get used to this," Father Felix said, gesturing to a table of breads, jams, and Martha's muffin treats.

"Yeah, we do all right," Father Tim said absently. He dug into his food and for long minutes the two kept silent. Father Felix busied himself buttering the top half of a muffin.

The young priest put his food away quickly, then he sat back. "I've been meaning to ask you something," he said, "something a little personal, if it's okay."

"Shoot," Father Felix said, reconciled to questions of this sort. It came with his penance.

"Yeah, well," Father Tim said hesitantly, "it's more about me than you, or maybe about the both of us."

"What's on your mind?" Father Felix said, layering jam on the muffin. "Want this?" he asked, offering it to his young boss.

Father Tim shook his head. "It's about women."

"Ah," said Father Felix, biting into Martha's specialty, "now you've come to the right guy."

"No, seriously," Father Tim said with a crack of smile at this priest's simplicity. The young priest got up and glanced down the hall, listening to the vacuum running in the rear bedroom. He sat back down, and leaning forward, lowered his voice, "I think I'm having some difficulty of my own here."

"With a woman?" Father Felix said, putting a touch of jam on the other half of his muffin.

"With a woman."

Father Felix looked around. "You know," he said, getting up, "Let's go into your office."

The younger priest got on his feet. "We can use Lou's," he said.

When the two of them were settled, Father Felix, coffee and muffin in hand, looked at the younger priest. "You were saying?"

"I've been thinking about this," Father Tim said. "Can a priest be on intimate terms with a woman? I don't mean physically, but can they get close, you know, in other ways?"

"What do you mean by close?"

Father Tim shook his head and made a face. "I'm not talking about anything physical." He hesitated, adding, "A guy needs friendships, no? Some intimacy in his life."

"With a woman?"

"Yeah, that too."

"Well," Father Felix said, "priests have close friends, some of whom can be women. Why not? Priests have mothers. What greater intimacy is there?"

Father Tim looked away. "I was thinking of something else," he said. "A relation with someone who, you know, is looking for companionship herself, for someone to be with, not physically, just to be close to. Someone you can open your heart and mind to. I think you know what I'm getting at."

"I guess I do," Father Felix said finishing off the muffin and absently licking his fingers.

"Right," Father Tim said, observing him. "I'd like to know what you think. Like, is it plainly wrong for me to want to spend time with a particular woman?"

He paused, and the older priest waited.

"Look, I'll be frank," Father Tim went on. "There's a young lady in our parish. She's got some serious problems, emotional problems, and I've been trying to help her. In the process, you know, maybe not so surprisingly, I've become drawn to her. I know there's probably some sort of physical thing operating too; she is really quite attractive, far as looks go, but it's not that exactly. I just like being with her."

The older priest looked at him quizzically and said nothing.

The young priest went on, "What's a man of the cloth supposed to do with these, you know, these feelings. From what you've been through, I mean. Are we supposed to just slam the door on it?"

Father Felix nodded and took a sip of coffee. "What's her name?"

"Monica."

"You're still just friends?"

"Not even that," Father Tim said.

"Is she drawn to you too?"

"She needs something, but I'm hardly it," Father Tim said glumly. "I'm the one with the lump in his throat."

Father Felix put his coffee down. "I guess you know the drill about things like that." The older priest hesitated, regarding the young priest across from him. After a pause, he said, "You know I lost my parish?"

"I'd heard."

Father Felix nodded. He knew his story was no secret. "I went to a monastery, a thousand miles from here," he went on. "I got to know a monk there, an older guy, Father Stan, all shriveled up with the worst arthritis. But to me he was a giant." Father Felix shook his head and sort of half chuckled, "He's the one who got me through my troubles born of a needy woman."

"To say nothing of one's own needs," Father Tim said.

"And one's own," the older priest repeated.

Father Felix became pensive, and again for a while neither of them spoke. Then he glanced up, "Would you like to know what this monk told me?"

Father Tim looked back at him with guarded eyes, letting the question hang.

Father Felix laughed a little. "I don't really know if he was holy or not, but my monk was plenty wise, and a very funny guy, I must say. We talked about these very things, too, a lot, just as we're doing here. His perspective on all this was pretty fascinating. He'd quote Christ's words, that we were to *love one another*, and he said our problem is, simply speaking, we don't, we don't dare, or if we do, we do it in some half-hearted way with our brakes on. It's all very true, he'd say, love is a risky business, especially for us priests when it comes to women. But the solution, and my monk said this over and over, the solution can never be *not* to love. That can't be right. No, we are called to love, us priests especially, so the way to love must also be there for us. And he insisted the way to love is right in front of us, in all its simplicity, even if it's the most difficult thing in the world. We're to love one another *as Our Lord loved us*, as he loved Mary Magdalene, for one."

The older priest paused, wondering if any of this was getting to the young priest before him.

"We talked about this business of intimacy too," he went on. "Father Stan liked to quote Our Lord in his great priestly prayer, that we would all be one with each other just as he and the Father are one. He used to laugh and slap his knee and say, *'Anything more intimate than that?'"*

Father Tim made a face. "Yeah, and we've taken that to mean we have to be *nice* to each other."

Father Felix looked at him with a nod. "I'll tell you one thing in particular he said to me, about his own personal difficulties in this business. He told other priests of this too, so I think I can share it with you. Maybe it will mean something to you. He said, as a young man he always wanted God, wanted to be holy, and he knew early on he might have a vocation. But he had this other want too. He used to dream of finding a woman who wanted to be holy too, but a real woman, someone he could embrace, knowing that, when they held each other that way, they would also be loving God, and God would be loving them, like a holy triangle. When he became a priest, that youthful dream of his got tucked away. But it never really died."

Father Felix reflected for a moment on his words, then he continued, "He didn't tell us much about this, but I gather there was a woman who came into his life, someone who must have felt the same way he did. It had nothing to do with physical intimacy, not at all, not initially. They were just very close."

Father Felix looked at his young counterpart. "Apparently it didn't exactly end that way."

"Yeah, right," Father Tim said dryly.

"So there's our problem in a nutshell, right?" the older priest said, looking into eyes that kept themselves back. "We priests have been formed with years of philosophy and theology. We wind up with all the right ideas and know how to think straight. But what about the heart? How is that to be taken care of? You're absolutely right, Tim. It's perfectly natural to crave someone to love, someone who is like you, someone with your tastes, your longings, someone who will love you back. You remember what Adam cried when he saw Eve that first time. *At last!*"

"Yeah," Father Tim said, "and what Adam got is not for us."

"Well, you're right, of course. That's what we gave up," Father Felix replied with an easy smile. "But, as you say, we still have to contend with the heart, one way or the other. Father Stan was right. Our job is to find out how. The trouble is we're afraid to even talk about these things. Nobody wants to go there. We see disorders right away, but Adam's cry had nothing to do with sex, you know. It had to do with his loneliness. God surely is no stranger to the heart. He knew Adam's need. And he sees our need. Christ is the New Adam, right? And we're called to be like him. *To love one another as he loved us.*"

Father Tim shook his head. "That's all fine theology, wonderful, but where does it get us, really?"

"I don't have ready answers, Tim," Father Felix said. "God knows I'm not your model. But I believe that Christ meant what He said, and that we're supposed to find out what that is. Intimacy doesn't have to be physical. It could be just in a look. What'd we read in the *Song of Solomon*? *Withdraw thine eyes from me for they make me soar aloft.*"

The young priest had to smirk. "That must be why we're taught custody of the eyes."

"Listen, Tim," Father Felix said, "the intimacy Christ calls us to is pure and holy. It's the intimacy He has with his Father. Is there greater intimacy than that?"

The older priest fell silent. "It doesn't have to be with this woman, Tim," he said finally. "Christ after all was a man. In any case, you don't go out and hunt for it. It has to find you. It has to be given, like Eve was given. And it has to be holy. You *can* find it sometimes just in a glance."

"Yeah, right," Father Tim said with one of his dry, ironic half laughs.

"Ah, Tim, but if you saw Christ in that glance, you would. How about the disciples? Didn't they leave their wives and their boats and tax tables, just because of what they saw when Christ looked at them?"

Father Tim peered at the older priest and said, "Can I ask you something?"

"Sure," said Father Felix, regarding his empty cup.

"If you don't mind my saying so," the young priest said, "you strike me as someone who is pretty much at peace with himself. Is it because you've found that—" he laughed, "that transcendent glance you spoke of?"

"In a way, yes."

"I take it not in the color of some woman's eyes this time."

"Well," Father Felix said, "I found it with this monk, Father Stan."

"Really?"

"You know, Tim," Father Felix went on, "we used to laugh a lot. There's chemistry when two people really have a good laugh. It can bond you. Best of all, though, we just liked being quiet together, as if the silences were holy somehow. But you know, other times all we had to do was catch each other's eye and we'd start grinning like two idiots."

Father Tim abruptly got to his feet. The younger priest seemed unready to absorb any of this.

"Listen," Father Felix said looking up at him. "What did the Evangelist John write? *Beloved, let us love one another.* We hear these words, but they just slip past us. You're right. We take it to mean we have to be *nice*." The older priest laughed. "For sure that's not what Our Lord had in mind exactly."

"Yeah," Father Tim said, "but that's not for us in this vale of tears."

"No, Tim, it will happen. The Father will give what his Son asked for. How can it be otherwise?"

He got up rather shakily as the younger priest moved to leave. The young priest had to reach out to steady him for a moment.

Father Tim hesitated at the door. "Were you ever tempted to stay there?" he asked. "In the monastery, with your monk? You were there so long."

"No," Father Felix said simply. "I knew I was to come back. Once I'd got what I needed."

He joined the young priest at the office door. "Tim," he said, "do you know what it really means to be forgiven?"

"Is this a serious question?"

"What could be more serious?" Father Felix said with an easy smile.

"We're all forgiven, aren't we?" Father Tim answered, a hint of annoyance in his tone. "That's what we sell here, if you don't mind my putting it that way."

"You can, but forgiven for what?"

"For being human, I suppose. For being what we are."

"Which is?"

"I don't know," the younger priest said, moving to get away. "Maybe, you're right. Maybe for not loving enough."

Father Felix seemed satisfied with that.

6

Several mornings later Father Felix had the nine o'clock but curiously, after Mass, the older priest failed to show up in the rectory for the breakfast Martha had laid out for him.

"I don't know where he is, Father," Martha said to the acting pastor when he came out from his office expecting to find him. "He hardly eats anything anyway," she said looking at the food she had laid out for him, adding, "I don't think he's too well."

Just then Martha's Paul came into the kitchen carrying a shopping bag in each hand. "Went to the store for my mother," he explained to the face that fell at the sight of him. "Your cuisine," he added, plunking the bags down on the counter.

Father Tim turned for his office. Paul abruptly called after him, "By the way, Father, I saw your friend at Mass this morning," adding with a laugh, "Maybe you can teach me how to pronounce her last name. It's too Polish for me."

Father Tim ignored him, but he switched course and headed toward the door leading to the church. Looking over at Martha, he said, "I'll see if he's all right."

"He's talking to her," Paul said. "I saw them go into the cry room."

Father Tim stopped at this revelation, spoke not a word and retreated to his office.

When he emerged half an hour later, there was no Felix, but Paul was still hanging around.

"I wanted to speak with him," Paul said defending his presence. "About his homily this morning. It was quite interesting."

Father Tim was about to go over to the church but he hesitated. "How do you mean?" he said.

"He talked about hell." When Father Tim looked at him doubtfully, he added, "You know, the justice of God."

Having caught the priest's attention, the young upstart hurried on, "He said that you can't understand a thing about forgiveness if you don't think that hell and punishment are real. That's pretty good, isn't it?" he said.

"I suppose it is," Father Tim said.

"Yeah," Martha's son said. "He's no liberal. That surprised me about him."

Seeing the acting pastor hang back at the door, he went on, "You know," he said, "some there this morning seemed pretty put off about the homily." Paul added with a laugh, "All anyone wants to hear nowadays is that God loves them."

"And he does," Father Tim said.

Paul could see he would be wise to leave.

A short while later Father Felix came in from the church, his step uncharacteristically alive. Finding Father Tim at the kitchen table, he smiled brightly, "I just spent an hour with the luckiest woman in the world." When he saw the expression in the younger priest's face he added, "Your friend Monica is an angel."

Father Tim changed the subject. "I hear you scared the ladies this morning," he said flatly.

"I did?"

"With your talk about hell."

Father Felix seemed surprised at the tone. "I don't think I used that word," he said with a smile. "I spoke about God's justice, that's true, but only so I could talk about his mercy."

"Well, I hear you had some of them terrorized."

"I don't terrorize," Father Felix said quietly. "Our job is to save souls from terror."

"The wrath of God," Father Tim said with a frown. "We don't talk that way anymore."

"I realize that," Father Felix said. "But don't you think maybe we should, once in a while?"

"Says who?"

"Listen, Tim," Father Felix said. "When the infant Jesus was presented at the temple, what did Simeon prophesy? This child would be for the falling and rising of many. That's our job, right? To keep souls from falling."

"By talking about mercy, not hell," Father Tim said bluntly.

"Exactly, Tim. Exactly. But how can you talk of mercy if there's no hell? We have to face reality. The Apostle Paul did. He said we were to work out our salvation with fear and trembling, no?"

"That's just not the way we speak nowadays," Father Tim said more evenly now. "Not even the pope."

"Maybe he will, one of these days. The Apostle certainly did. By the way, Tim," Father Felix said, seeking calmer waters, "I think you'll find this dear parishioner of yours far more peaceful now."

"Well, I'm glad to hear it," Father Tim said quietly. "She's been to hell and back."

They both had to laugh at the remark. It seemed to clear the air.

"Hey, wait a minute," the younger priest said suddenly. "You're not wearing your cross!"

"I gave it to your friend," Father Felix said.

"*She's* not going to *wear* it?" Father Tim said, incredulous.

"I hardly think so. It doesn't have to be worn."

"Amazing," Father Tim said shaking his head.

"You know, Tim," the older priest said, "I got that cross from my monk. And he got it from someone before him. The legend has it that it was made of hardwood from the Mount of Olives, and that it's been handed down from one soul to the next over the centuries. It's meant to be passed on."

The younger priest pointed to the other's chest and added with a little laugh, "You don't look yourself without it, somehow."

"Well, it's *hers* now," Father Felix said affably.

"Interesting stuff," the young priest allowed.

Then he excused himself and walked away. The acting pastor had things to do.

7

Earlier, on that same day, as soon as Father Felix had left the altar after celebrating the nine o'clock Mass, the lovely figure of this woman, Monica, appeared in the doorway of the sacristy. "Excuse me, Father," she said. "May I speak with you?"

The old priest, about to take off his alb, looked over at Monica and nodded. "Just a sec," he said, pulling the long, white garment over his head. He hung it in the closet, ran a hand over his thinning gray hairs and then, looking out into the nave of the church, he turned off the lights, except in the back where a little knot of parishioners had yet to leave.

"We can go into the children's cry room," he said leading her out of the sacristy.

After they settled in, Father Felix briefly studied the woman beside him. "So now," he said, "what's on your mind?" He could see something was brewing.

"Father," she said, "you spoke so much about God's justice." Monica hesitated, looking for the right words. "I can't put that together with love," she said at length. "I know you tried, but they seem so . . . opposed."

Father Felix did not answer her right away. She had to be the one disturbing the conscience of the young assistant at St. Andrew's. It was understandable. She was uncommonly lovely, not exactly beautiful perhaps, in the strict classic sense, but with the kind of stunning head-to-toe appearance that made you look again, even if you didn't want to.

"Can I ask you something?" he said at length. "It might help me to address your difficulty. You remember I talked about fathers this morning, how a good father has special responsibility not only to love but to exercise justice, too." After a pause, he asked, "Were you by any chance close to your father?"

Monica shook her head. "I don't remember anything about my father," she said dryly. "I was too young," she added without explaining herself.

"I'm sorry," Father Felix said. He fell silent for a moment, then said, "May I ask you something else?"

"I guess that depends, Father," Monica said with a faint toss of her head. Her tone was not inviting.

"Talks with priests do get personal sometimes, don't they," the old priest said with a little laugh.

"I suppose they do," she said shifting in her chair. This wasn't the conversation she had in mind.

"You don't have to answer this," he said, "but it might get to the heart of your difficulty."

"I'm sorry, Father," she apologized. "I'm still wary of people trying to help me." She looked at the priest and sort of smiled.

"I just wondered," he said. "You say you have trouble with the idea of God's justice. I suppose you mean by that *God* as a *judge*."

"Yes."

"I gather you feel that if God loves us, He shouldn't judge us, right?"

"Yes," she said, "exactly. Didn't Jesus Christ say we were not supposed to judge? Why does *God* want to judge us?"

Father Felix nodded. "That's a valid question," he said, "But I have one, too. I think it may get at what you're really asking."

He looked at her as if seeking permission to proceed, then he said, "I wonder if you believe in hell, that there *is* such a place?"

An odd look spread almost instantly across Monica's face. After a moment she said simply, "I have trouble with that."

"It's not surprising. Everyone does," Father Felix said. "But can I ask you if there's some particular reason."

Monica hesitated. "To go into that," she said flatly, "I'd have to tell you my life's story." Then she added, "I don't usually do that." She sat up as if wanting to leave.

The old priest stretched out his hand. "Let me tell you something about myself, then," he said. "It may help you." Father Felix fixed his gaze on this woman beside him, his eyes softening. "When I was your age," he said, "as a young priest, I felt just as you do. I never gave these dark thoughts a moment. You should have heard me. God loves us no matter what, right? Of course, it's true, He does. Thank heaven He does. But there was never a word about his judgment of us."

Father Felix hesitated, unsure he should continue. But his homily had opened a wound. "That all changed for me," he went on, "when something happened in my priestly life, something serious, something that shouldn't have happened."

Again another pause, then, "That's when thoughts of judgment, hell, of eternal banishment, all began to plague me. I was at a point where I had to deal with it."

Father Felix paused again, a long pause. Was something as personal as this going to help her? He wasn't sure. "Hell is real, you know," he said after a while. "The Apostle gave us wise advice when he told us to work out our salvation with fear and trembling." He chuckled some and held up the cross resting on his chest. "That's why I wear this," he said. "It keeps me in focus."

"Are you afraid of God?" Monica said, seemingly forgetting she was talking to a priest.

"No, thanks be to heaven," Father Felix said simply, suppressing a grin. "But, you know, there *is* a place for holy fear. Scripture tells us fear is the beginning of wisdom."

Monica said quietly, "I'm sorry, Father. I think I'm the one who's afraid."

"Then you're on your way to wisdom," Father Felix said with a nodding smile.

THE HEART HATH ITS REASONS

"I wish," she said.

Father Felix waited. He'd said all he felt he could. He'd already talked enough that morning. He looked at Monica, "Is there anything else," he said at length.

She hesitated, as if trying to make up her mind. Then, abruptly, she said, "I was in the hospital recently. That was serious too." Then, after another pause, she added, "They tell me I almost died."

Father Felix nodded.

After a moment she went on, "I had a dream as I lay there, in the hospital. I had it three times in fact, three nights in a row. An old priest stood by my bedside. I couldn't see his face very clearly." She began to shake her head. "For all I know it could have been you."

"How would I get in your dream?" he said almost laughing.

"I don't know, Father. He was an elderly priest, that's all I recall."

"Did he speak to you?"

"He just kept looking at me, saying nothing, just looking. And then as he'd turn to leave he'd say, *My daughter, remember that it will be forever and ever.*" Monica shuddered. "I had that dream three nights in a row."

Monica peered at the priest. "You remind me of him," she said.

Father Felix had to chuckle at that, but then fell into pensive silence. After a while the old priest looked up. "I've never told this to anyone," he said, "but, you know, at every Mass I celebrate, without fail, I ask God to receive this holy sacrifice for one soul, to save that soul from gnashing teeth for all eternity." He stopped for a moment and then added, "It's true what you heard in your dream. Whatever one's fate, it's going to be forever and ever."

Monica snapped at this, "Why does there have to be a hell? Why can't God just forgive? People forgive, don't they?"

"God does forgive. That's what He's all about."

"Then why is there hell?"

"Hell is for those who don't want God, don't want his forgiveness. Their attitude is 'What's to forgive?' There are legions like this nowadays."

"But can't God forgive them for that, too?"

"He could, I suppose, but not without doing violence to his justice."

"That's just what I don't understand," Monica said, leaning forward. "God's justice. It seems so cruel."

"Well, look at it this way, Monica." Father Felix stopped. "Your name is Monica, isn't it?"

"Yes, Father," she said with a faint flush. "I'm sorry, I should have introduced myself."

"I felt I knew you," he said smiling. "From Father Tim. He thinks so well of you."

"Yes," she said, looking down.

"Anyway," Father Felix went on, "if you think about justice, it has to do with the relationship between two parties, right? That relationship can be either just or unjust. Justice is when the parties honor each other's rights, give each other his or her due. That's clear enough, right?"

"I understand that, Father, but . . ."

"And," he persisted, "if one party takes something that belongs to the other party, that would be an injustice, right? Suppose a man just ups and takes his neighbor's car. The world would be a sorry place if that sort of thing were tolerated."

"Okay, Father," she said, "I get the point. But if someone takes something that belongs to you, you can still forgive that person, isn't that also true?"

"Yes, of course. And that's the way it is with us, on God's side of the bargain. After all, parents don't stop loving their son just because he robbed a bank. No, they still love him, but justice also has to be dealt with, no? The son can't just keep the money he stole. It's no different with us and God. We've stolen something of great value from him—ourselves—we belong to him, after all. And yes, he wants to forgive us for that sin, absolutely, but what was stolen still has to be given back. That's only just. Mercy has its part, but justice does too."

Father Felix looked pointedly at Monica. "Maybe you understand that's where the Cross comes in? To satisfy the justice part."

Monica remained silent.

Father Felix made a little gesture and went on, "And then there's this other thing, too," he said. "The Father has afforded *us* rights also. We have the right to deny his claim to us. We can even deny He exists. So you see, justice involves rights on both sides. In justice we're obliged to give God what He wants, but in the name of that same justice He's obliged to do the same for us. So if what we want is anything but God, what can God in justice do? He has to oblige us, but He warns us what that will mean."

Father Felix had to laugh. "Maybe even through an old priest like me."

"But why is it forever?" Monica broke in. "Why does it have to be that way?"

Father shrugged his shoulders. "That's just the way it is. God is eternal, no? Life with Him is eternal. It has to be. And so must life apart from Him."

The old priest stopped, eyeing her discomfort.

"I don't want to go there," she said.

"Then you won't."

Monica smiled lamely and looked away.

The old priest regarded the woman across from him, silent, her head cast down. He watched her reach for a tissue. "Monica," he said softly, "do you sometimes look at the Cross?"

Monica, not looking up, shook her head.

The old priest took her by the hand and, getting no resistance, led her back out into the semi-dark, empty nave of the church.

He led her up to the foot of the sanctuary and, pointing to the life-size crucifix hanging behind the altar, he said, "Tell me, what do you see when you look at Him?"

"I don't really like to," she said.

"But you must, you know. You really must."

"It's so . . . brutal."

"Because hell is brutal," the old priest said.

"I'm sorry Father," Monica said. "It just seems so, so unconnected, to where I am."

The old priest said nothing to this.

Monica sank down in the front pew. She seemed short of breath. "How can anyone understand it," she said.

Father Felix slid in next to her and together they sat there, neither of them speaking. Monica dabbed at her eyes. She noticed mascara on her tissue.

In the quiet they fell to gazing up at the only thing there to look at, the huge Cross looming before them.

After a while Father Felix said, "You know, Our Lord foresaw that many would say *no* to Him. It pained him more than the nails. But that was their call and there was nothing more He could do to save them."

She sat up straight to meet his eyes. "No one talks the way you do, Father," she said. "It's so, so . . . foreign to me. Priests talk about the 'good news' of the Gospel. Now you say the Gospel has this bad news too."

"Yes, it does," he said simply. "There's the gnashing of teeth, remember. But it doesn't have to be that way. God has done everything He can to spare us that fate, that timeless, endless gnashing of teeth. That's what this Cross is saying to us, right here and now."

Again a long silence, broken finally as the old priest asked her, "Tell me, Monica, are you baptized?" He did not recall her receiving communion that morning.

"I guess so, Father," Monica said looking over at him. "Growing up I always thought I was Catholic. I even went to parochial school for a year. But my mother never took me to church. She never talked about religion."

"Well, there are church records. Father Tim can look into that. You ought to have some instruction, anyway."

"Could you do that?"

"We'll see."

It seemed they'd said enough. They sat there side by side in the dim light of the nave, not speaking. The dark, empty church at that moment seemed flooded with a perfect stillness. Facing them at the back of the unlit sanctuary, the flicker of the red vigil lamp announced the mystery in the tabernacle, and above, on the wall, the life-size Cross, another, still greater mystery. In the shadows, the figure of the Crucified One looked to be peering down at them. The two sat there in that stillness, each in their own way taking it in.

"Do you see how much He loves you?" the old priest said at length.

Monica responded with a barely discernible movement of her body, but she said nothing.

The priest said softly, "Look at Him. He's asking for you."

Monica could not bring herself to reply.

Another lengthy silence. Then Father Felix leaned over towards her and began to relate a story.

"I knew a man once," he said, "a man who was literally knocked for a loop by a certain woman. This happened the very first moment he laid eyes on her. The young lady for her part didn't even know he existed, but he artfully managed to introduce himself, and with persistence, over time, he got to dating her, wining and dining her at the best places. The woman was quite beautiful in his eyes, and he found himself dreaming of her day and night. His love for her grew and grew until he got to a place where he couldn't imagine any kind of life without her. He had to make her his own. So he set about doing everything he could to win her heart, even changing things in his own life, just to please her. And it seemed to him that he was getting somewhere. Finally, when he thought the moment was right, he took everything he had and purchased a magnificent diamond ring. And with that ring in hand, he arranged for a candlelight dinner in a special restaurant where he would declare his love and ask her to be his. But that evening when he went to pick her up, she wasn't home. He waited and waited outside her place, but she never came back that night. Had something happened to her? You can imagine his concern and confusion. But that confusion became utter devastation the next day when he learned the love of his life had gone off with someone else."

Father Felix looked over at the woman beside him. "Christ is like that man," he said.

Monica said nothing. She seemed so alone at that moment.

"Monica," the priest went on, "you are a lovely woman. You must have had many suitors. Forgive me if I ask another personal question. Have you ever been in love, really in love with someone?"

Father Felix reached to touch her hand. "I'm sorry," he said softly. "You don't have to answer that."

Monica slowly turned to the old priest and said, "Father, . . . is it okay to go to confession? For me, I mean."

After a flicker of hesitation, flashing through his mind what she had said about her upbringing, about parochial school, about her probable baptism, the old priest said,

"Why yes, of course." Turning to face her, he said, "We can right here, if you'd like."

"Help me, Father," she said. "I don't remember how to do this."

"That's no problem," he said leaning back. "Just tell me what's weighing on you." The priest closed his eyes and slowly made the sign of the cross. "Go ahead now. God will hear you."

The confession was full and lengthy, discharging a life of painful memories, of intimate relations that were pointless and untruthful, of hurts both inflicted and suffered, of emptiness, pills and depression. And then the despairing act that almost took her life. Father Felix once or twice asked about some point, delicately, always in a voice that could only encourage and reassure. When finally she concluded, "That's everything, Father, everything I can remember," he coached her with the act of contrition. He had her repeat each phrase after him: *I am heartily sorry . . . because I fear the loss of heaven and the pains of hell . . . because I have offended Thee, who art all good and worthy of all my love.*

Following the absolution, the two remained together in the pew, Monica with her head down, praying her penance as the priest had instructed. When she looked up, eyes glowing, Father Felix leaned over and lightly kissed her on the forehead—a kiss of peace he was to explain—and in reply Monica threw her arms around him. Moments later, breaking away, the old priest took up the cross he was wearing, raised it up over his head and handed it to her.

"I would like you to have this," he said resting the hardwood in her hands.

"Really, Father?" she said flustered, gazing down at it.

"It's for you now," he said.

"But it's yours," she said. "Father, I can't . . ."

"No, my dear, take it. It's meant to be passed on." He smiled and added, "You don't have to wear it, not as I did, not at all. Just keep it with you. Keep it until you have a reason to pass it on yourself. It's been in many, many hands before I received it. And you won't be the last to carry it, I'm sure. But for now, my friend, it's for you."

Just then the noise of a door closing at the front entrance of the church reminded Father Felix that he still had to lock up. Incidents of vandalism in some of the parishes had made locking up obligatory right after the nine o'clock.

8

Early that afternoon of the same day, Father Felix stuck his head in his acting boss's office. "Martha said you wanted to see me."

"Yeah," said Father Tim. "Thanks."

Father Felix took a seat and waited. It was more than obvious to him something was amiss.

"I don't know how to go about this," Father Tim said, twisting somewhat in his seat.

"About what?" Father Felix said.

"You probably don't realize it," the young priest began. "Some of our parishioners have, you know . . . well, let's say they're complaining about you."

The older priest looked at his young boss, waiting.

"Your homily this morning, for one thing." These words did not come easily. "Some of them found it a bit . . . unsettling maybe is the right word."

Father Felix smiled. "There's plenty in our religion that's unsettling, no?"

"It's not just that," Father Tim said. "You know what the problem is, Felix. I don't have to bring up that old matter."

The older priest said nothing, his eyes fixed on his young superior.

"And then there's the incident this morning."

"My homily?"

"No, after Mass. You were with this Monica. Someone was bothered by what they saw."

"I don't understand," Father Felix said. "We had a good talk, a wonderful talk. I spoke to you about that earlier."

"Felix," Father Tim said, taking a deep breath, "I understand all that. The problem is how it appears."

"How what appears?" Father Felix said fighting off annoyance.

"Someone saw you there in the pews," the priest blurted out. "I'm sorry, Felix. This isn't easy for me."

Felix had to laugh. "Ah, okay, I see. Yes," he said, "at the end there was a heartfelt embrace, even a kiss of peace." He laughed again. "I have to admit that." Then he added, "Your friend made a great leap forward this morning. She's probably never been so happy in her entire life."

"It's the appearance, Felix," Father Tim said. "Coupled with everything else."

"Coupled with everything else," the older priest repeated in a quiet, weary voice.

For several long moments they sat there peering at each other, neither uttering a word.

"So what are you saying, Tim?"

"There's some kind of parish petition in the works, to the Chancery, about you."

"About a kiss of peace?" the older priest said, half amused.

"No, Felix, it's hardly that." Again a long pause, then, "People here just don't understand you. And I'd like to spare you more grief with the bishop. You don't need that." He added, "I'm sorry. It's just not working out."

"You're asking me to leave?"

"I thought we could tell the Chancery it was your health. There's no need to open up old wounds. Besides, Felix, you haven't been well. We're worried about you. Martha says you hardly eat."

The older priest had to smile at these incongruities. But he nodded, "There's some truth in that part at least." After a moment, he added, "More than I've let on."

"How do you mean?"

"The doctors tell me I haven't much time."

Father Tim just stared at him.

"They give me a few months, maybe a bit more if I'm lucky," Father Felix said simply.

The younger priest sat back, stunned. "I had no idea," he uttered. "Why would they send you here?"

"I never let on," the older priest said. "I suppose I should have," he allowed, "but you see, Tim, I wanted to get back into a parish, even for a time as brief as this." Father Felix spoke softly, without any hint of hard feeling, at peace already with his new circumstance.

"I'm truly sorry," Father Tim said, shaking his head, at a loss for anything more. Then he said, "I wish our people had shorter memories."

Father Felix sat there quietly for a few moments, letting it all sink in. Finally, he said, "Effective when, Tim? As of right now?"

"Might as well," he said lamely.

"Will you call the Chancery?" Father Felix said, adding, "I'd prefer that."

"Of course. I'll take care of it."

They sat there exchanging looks, aware they were abruptly now in different worlds.

Finally Father Felix stood up. "Tim, before I go and pack up my things, would you be good enough to hear my confession? I haven't been since coming here."

Father Tim did a double take, but he quickly recovered, and moments later two priests closed their eyes, one with head held low, the other with arm raised, slowly, deliberately forming a sign of the cross.

Later, as he stood in the rectory vestibule with his thin bags, waiting for the cab, the older priest regarded the young priest a final time. "Tim," he said, his fingers reaching out to touch him, "just remember these two things. One, we don't learn to love well by *not* loving. And two, the most important thing, Our Lord's in charge of all this. If we give him half a chance, his prayer to the Father will win the day."

The sound of an auto horn caught their attention. Father Tim took the old priest's bags and helped him out to the taxi waiting at the curb. There was a brief clasping of hands. Father Felix said, "Bless you, Tim," and the younger priest thanked him for his service. It embarrassed him that he hadn't inquired where Felix would be staying. It was late for that now.

And that was that.

Reflecting later, Father Tim knew that, despite everything, he'd come to have uncommon respect for this aging compadre. The acting pastor could not say what it was exactly, but he'd never met anyone like Felix Cooper, priest or otherwise. He wondered if he was witnessing the misfortunes of a man who might just have the makings of a saint. That just might be.

9

Ten days later Monica came to the rectory to see Father Tim. It goes without saying he was more than glad to see her. He noticed at once that she seemed more relaxed. Even the sound of her voice was different.

"We haven't seen you for a while," he said, leading her into his office.

"Father," she said, once they settled in. "I'm leaving. I wanted you to know."

"You're leaving the parish?"

"No, Father. I'm going away."

"I'm sorry to hear that," he said, struggling with a face that said rather more.

Monica flushed at this. "I wanted to thank you, for all you did for me."

"What did I do?" he said, recovering. "Besides liking to talk to you. Too much probably." He knew he needn't have added that.

Monica glanced down at this, then, looking up she said, "You know Father Felix is leaving."

"No, I didn't."

"He's going back to his monastery. You know he's not well."

"That makes sense," Father Tim said, nodding. "Someone's going to have to look after him."

"I'm going with him," Monica said.

"That's good," he said. "He shouldn't be traveling alone."

"I'll be staying with him," she added.

"How do you mean? At the monastery?"

"I believe they have a guest house, Father. And I can be helpful . . . as his time nears. The abbot told him it would be okay."

"You and he have gotten pretty close," Father Tim said.

"Yes, Father. He's been catechizing me. He couldn't find any record of a baptism."

"I didn't realize that," Father Tim said quietly.

Monica suddenly became animated. "Father, can I tell you something I've been learning?"

"Sure."

"Well, it has to do with what happens when, you know, you kind of run into God head-on, like I did. Father Felix says it takes you to a new place, to a new under-standing, a new you."

"They call that conversion," Father Tim said.

"Yes, but there's this journey that has to come after-wards, isn't that right?"

The young priest nodded but had no ready reply.

"So, Father, it's true," she said, "I am going on a trip." She laughed, "In both senses."

The young priest could not keep from studying the woman so unexpectedly there before him. "Whatever's going on," he said, "I can see it's changing you." What he could not say is that she seemed more captivating than ever.

"I've been very blessed, Father."

This was followed by an awkward pause where nei-ther could seem to find words.

The young priest got up and came around the desk. "We're going to miss you around here." He spoke this rather more coolly than he should have, and he realized it confused her. He smiled at her half apologetically, and then, looking at his watch, he said, "I'm sorry to cut this short, but I really have to run."

"Of course, Father," Monica said, rising. Hesitating for an embarrassed instant, she reached out to shake his hand, and with that she departed.

10

Late one morning, two months later, the housekeeper, Martha, slipped into the acting pastor's office and closed the door. "Father," she said quietly, "that woman with the Polish name, Monica Tresh . . . ," she stalled. "I can never pronounce it."

"Trześniewska."

"Right," she said with a helpless laugh. "She's here to see you."

"She's here?" Father Tim said getting up. But he sat back at once.

"Shall I bring her in?"

"Have her wait," he said. Then, "I won't be long."

"I'll tell her, Father."

The acting pastor slumped back and closed his eyes. A few minutes later he had Martha bring her in.

"You're back," he said rising to his feet.

"I had to see you," Monica said.

"You know," he said, brightening, "we thought we'd never lay eyes on *you* again." He pointed to a chair. "I'm awfully glad you're here," he said.

They sat facing each other for a few moments, exchanging looks and broad smiles of pleasure.

"You look good," he said.

"I ought to," she said with a laugh. "After they got through with me."

"They?"

"You know, Father Felix. And his monk, Father Stanislaw."

"Another Pole I take it," Father Tim said with a laugh.

"Yes," she said, laughing with him.

"You were there the whole time?"

"Yes, the whole time. I was at his bedside the night Father Felix passed away."

"Felix died," the young priest said quietly, his eyes wandering off. Looking back he said, "I'm sorry. I hadn't heard."

After absorbing this, his eyes fell back on the woman across from him. "Whatever happened out there has done you a world of good."

"Father Stan taught me so much," she said. "They both did."

"I'd heard about that monk."

"He's different," she said. "I never met anyone like him."

"In what way?"

"Like, he doesn't really seem to dwell in his own skin." She shook her head. "I can't explain it."

The young priest merely raised an eyebrow.

"He's the abbot now," she went on, "despite his being so crippled. He just took me in. He even let me stay right there."

"In the monastery?"

"In the infirmary, Father. To help out with Father."

"That was very good of you."

"That's how I got to know Father Stan, too. Can I tell you a little about what happened?"

"Sure, of course, please do."

"Well," she said, "The very first time I met Father Stan, he just studied me—who was I—and then, right out of the blue, he asked me if I wanted to become holy. What could I say?" she said with a little laugh. "I just smiled at him and sort of nodded."

"Yeah," Father Tim half joked, "what does he expect you to say?"

"Then right away he asked me, 'Do you know how a person becomes holy?' I had to admit I hadn't a clue."

"He moves right in on you, doesn't he?" Father Tim said with a faint toss of his head.

"You know," she continued, "at first I couldn't tell if he was serious, his manner was so light. But I soon found out," she added with a quiet laugh. "But in a way, holiness is really very simple, isn't it Father?"

Father Tim seemed hardly to be following what she was saying. He had been so certain he would never see her again.

"Can I tell you what he said?" she went on, suddenly unsure of her footing. "What he taught me. About holiness."

"Oh, sure," he said, leaning back.

"Well," she began, glancing at the priest uncertainly, "he used to say that when it comes to our holiness, it's God who does the heavy lifting." She hesitated, glancing up to see if the priest would abide her going on this way. But she had reasons to persist.

She went on, "Father Stan said our job is to let God get a good grip on us. Then he'd laugh and say, 'But watch out. He's going to take you for a ride.'"

Again she hesitated. "That ride's not as easy as it sounds, is it, Father?" she said, peering at him.

"Right," the young priest said absently, reaching to shove some papers aside on his desk.

"Father," she said more quickly, "I have something I really need to ask of you, but I have to tell you about this holiness business first. About what I learned. Is it okay? It's terribly important to me."

"No problem," Father Tim said, shifting forward a little.

"It's a little involved," Monica said. "But please hear me." She took a deep breath, and then launched into the following account.

"Father Stan especially liked the metaphor of a *train* ride. He said the journey is long, past one station after another. You can get off at any one of these stops if you want, and he says most people do in fact. The first station has to do simply with God's existence, that there is a God and that he governs the universe. Father said a great many get off right here. They're just happy to know God's out there, like a giant plug that keeps the meaning of it all from draining out. Father Stan calls them bathtub theists."

"That's cute," Father Tim allowed.

"But if you stay on board," Monica pressed on gamely, "you go beyond just recognizing God's existence and all his cosmic power. You begin to think about Him as a person, what He's like. You want to learn about Him. You reflect on what He's done for you personally, you know, like your own heartbeat is a gift. And by the time you get to the next station you understand that God not only exists and is all-powerful, He is also good, that He is goodness itself, and that He's been good to you."

"A lot of people get off here also," Monica went on. "They're content knowing that God will take care of them. What more could anyone want? But some feel the need to answer to that goodness, to respond to it. There's something in them that wants to reply to God, to serve Him, to do his will. And so these particular passengers stay on board. The number now is a lot smaller."

She glanced uneasily at Father Tim, aware of this blatant reversal of their roles. "Is this tiring you, Father?"

"No, not at all," he said.

"It's just a metaphor," Monica said softly. "But it helped me so much."

"Hey, that makes it interesting," Father Tim said leaning forward more.

"So, anyway, Father," she began again, "as the train pulls away it starts out on a pretty happy note. The intention to do God's will brings with it a certain contentment, even if it may be hard at times." Monica looked at him. "Isn't that so, Father?"

"You bet."

"But then something happens along the way that begins to unsettle the ones still on board. It begins when they learn *what* exactly God's will *is* for them, what He in fact wants of them: *Be ye perfect as your heavenly Father is perfect.* At first, no one takes it too seriously, it seems just so unrealistic. But as the train moves on, they begin to understand that Our Lord really meant what He said. He wants our perfection, and not just human perfection, but the perfection of God Himself, *in us*. So, almost inevitably, one by one, most of the passengers conclude that this perfection is too idealistic and is simply not for them. Father Stan says it doesn't mean that these are not good people. They want to serve God, and they do, as well as they can. But perfection, well, they think that's for the saints. That's how they reason, and so the majority of these good people get off at the very next station."

"Can't exactly blame them," Father Tim said offhandedly.

"No, you're right, Father. But there's this much smaller number who want to go the whole way, to give God everything he asks for, so they stay on board. But then— this is the way Father Stan put it—once the train gets underway, everything begins to change, and it's not a change for the better as far as anyone can tell."

Monica took a full breath and went on, looking guardedly at the priest. "Almost at once, the train ascends a steep, rocky mountain and when the passengers look out, all they see is mist and deep chasms far below on either side. They become frightened. And then a great wind comes and shakes the train, making it feel like it could leave the track and end their lives. But the worst moments are not those outside but inside, taking place within these travelers. They find that no matter how hard they try, the perfection they seek lies beyond them, utterly, cruelly out of reach, and increasingly so. All they can see in themselves any more are their imperfections, their shortcomings, infidelities, the very absence of anything good. And they're supposed to become perfect with the perfection of God Himself! We can't do it! they cry. And so at the next station, discouraged to the bone, most all of them get off. They tried, they tried really hard, but perfect holiness is not for them. They feel they know that now for sure. So now only the tiniest handful remain on board, only a precious few."

Monica hesitated, glancing a bit lamely at Father Tim. "Am I getting too carried away, Father?" she said.

The priest gave her a tolerant smile. "It's OK."

She began again, "Father Stan calls these the *chosen ones*. Yes, it's true, he said, all these special souls can see now are their imperfections, and much worse, in fact. They feel as though this journey so far had actually been taking them backwards. But they don't get off, they stay on board anyway, hoping, trusting that the Lord would not ask something of them that was beyond reach. And these souls are rewarded for their trust and perseverance, because now, once the train gets under way, they are given a great new understanding, one that transforms everything. This happens, Father Stan says, because they gave up their own thoughts and listened. And what they heard—and Father Stan say's he heard it too—is there's only one way to please the Father."

Monica looked at Father Tim. "Father Stan told me what Our Lord actually said to him. It was just a few words. Would you like me to repeat them, Father?"

"Sure," Father Tim said.

Monica spoke them deliberately, distantly, as words not her own: *Now you know you can't please the Father by what you do by yourself. That is the blessed lesson. So now, let Me please the Father through you, with you, and in you.*

123

Color rushed to her face. "By the time the ride is over," she said, "the lucky ones who stayed the course become holy and perfect."

Monica glanced up shyly at the priest.

"I take it you're one of those who managed to hang in there," he said with a grin.

"Oh, Father," she said, throwing up both hands before her, shaking her head, "I'm no saint."

"Well, whatever," he said, "I'm impressed. You're not the same." He laughed a little. "Maybe I should go to that monastery myself, pick up some of these ideas."

"Father," she said, "it's not ideas, you know."

"Yeah, of course, you're right," he said weakly. What was getting to him had little to do with monasteries and metaphors. The changes in her were actually a little unsettling.

Just then the phone on his desk rang. Martha's voice explained that there was a call for his visitor. Some young man with another name she couldn't get. "It sounds terribly Polish," she said.

"There's a call for you," Father Tim said, coming out from behind his desk to hand her the phone. He headed towards the door.

Monica gestured for him to stop. Then into the phone she all but whispered, "Hi, Jan . . . Yes, yes, everything's fine . . . No, let me call you back, okay?" and she handed the phone over to the priest.

"Father," she said gathering herself. "I have something for you." She reached into her purse and took out the hardwood cross.

Holding it up, she said, "I think you recognize this, right?"

"I guess I do," he said. "Felix gave you that."

"Yes, Father. And it's for you now." Moving closer, she quickly draped it over his head.

Father Tim stepped back, grabbing the cross away from his chest. "What's this all about?" he said looking down at it, half annoyed.

"Please accept it, Father. It's meant for you now."

"Why me?" he said. "I don't get it."

"Father, I know you're supposed to have it. I'm certain of it."

Father Tim merely shook his head, still holding the cross away from him, in both hands. "I can't accept this," he said.

"Why Father? Maybe God wants you to have it."

Father Tim wanted to laugh. "Did He tell you that?"

"Well, not exactly. But . . . Father, it doesn't have to be worn. I certainly didn't. Just keep it close to you until, you know, someone else someday comes along who needs it more."

"Is that what you think, that I need this?" he said, still holding it out.

"Maybe it's me who needs it, Father," she said. "I mean that it's me who needs you to have it."

"You got me," he said shaking his head. "I appreciate the thought, but really, you know, I can't accept this." He started to take it off until she placed her hand on his.

"Wait, Father. Just hear me out, okay?"

The priest dropped his hands and sank back against

the desk. "Okay," he said stiffly. "Tell me. What's going on?"

"It's about that train to holiness, Father," she began. "Once those few passengers get the right idea about sanctity, about perfection, a lot of things still have to happen to them, like patience, perseverance, purity. Things that eluded them before, but now they're all gifts, right? Father, you know this better than I."

The young priest's mouth tightened. "The Church calls these *fruits* of the Spirit, not gifts."

"Thank you, Father. Anyway," she forged on, "do you know what the end of that train ride is? The last stop? What the end of holiness is? What the greatest fruit of all is?"

Father Tim remained silent. His body began rocking almost imperceptibly against the desk.

"It's love, Father, right?" she said quickly. "Not *our* love, but God's love. His love in us. Isn't that right? Isn't that the greatest gift?"

Feeling his impatience, she exclaimed with some force, "Father, I'm telling you all this for a reason. I feel there's unfinished business between us."

"How do you mean?" he said straightening up.

"Well," she said more meekly, "I knew how you felt about me. A woman always knows those things. But I couldn't respond. I've never been able to love back somehow. You must have felt it."

Quite possibly no one had ever witnessed the shade that flooded the young priest's face just then.

"I know you felt it," she said. "And I'm so sorry for my part in that . . . pain."

"Why are you telling me this?" he blurted. Then, calming, "I don't get it . . ."

"Father," Monica said quickly, "didn't Jesus tell us we are to love one another? Not in *our* way of loving, but in *his*." When she said this, she placed her palm on the cross and pressed it against him. "With *his* love," she said.

"Yeah," the priest said. "And how in God's name do you do that?"

Monica moved closer. "By taking the first step," she said, reaching for him and throwing her arms about him. He felt her warmth digging the ancient wood into his chest. For the briefest moment his hands touched her shoulders, then they dropped to his side.

"Why?" he cried, stepping back, his chest heaving.

"Because I want to love you back," she said softly, adding, "Because I want to trust love, *his* love."

Father Tim sank down on the chair she'd been on. "He's had some effect on you," he said catching his breath.

"On you too, Father."

"Maybe so," he said with half a laugh. "Maybe so."

Monica beamed. "God has been so very good to us."

"I was talking about Felix," he said with a funny smile, getting a grip on himself.

Then, after some wordless moments, Monica said, "You'll keep the cross?"

He took it in his hands and with a deep inhale he nodded, "Yeah, I'll keep it."

"Father, thank you. That's really what I came for." A

moment later she added, "But there's something else too. Something we need to ask of you."

Father Tim gazed up at her. "We?"

"Jan and I. The person who just called me." She blushed as she explained, "Jan and I are getting married."

Father Tim had to catch himself. Rising to his feet he said, "Now I know why you look so happy."

"Yes," she said. "And Father Felix was hoping to marry us. But then Father just wasn't able to. He blessed our wedding though, sort of in advance, from his sick bed. And he told us some beautiful things about what love is all about."

Father Tim said nothing to this.

"Father Stan offered to marry us," she continued, "But . . . we were hoping you would."

Father Tim began to laugh a bit uneasily. "You're full of surprises today," he said. Catching himself, he added, "Of course. I'd be absolutely happy to. Have you two set a date?"

"As soon as possible, Father."

"How soon is that?"

"Could you marry us now?"

"Are you serious?"

"Why not, Father. We got our license today. Jan is outside in the car."

"Hey, the Church requires a waiting period, you know. These things can't be rushed."

"We did all that," she threw in. "At the monastery, really."

After a moment, the priest said, "Your Jan is outside?"

"Yes, Father. With the rings."

Father Tim put his arm around Monica and drew her with him to the door. "I have to meet this lucky guy."

Martha the housekeeper, busy at the sink, glanced over as the two hurried by the kitchen. She noted that Father Tim seemed happy about something. She hadn't noticed the plain wooden cross swinging over the chest of St. Andrew's acting pastor.

11

It's two o'clock in the morning, two weeks later. Father Tim is dozing at the kitchen table waiting for his boss's arrival when, in the night's stillness, he awakens to the slam of a car door and outside a muffled voice. He rouses himself and goes out into the hallway just as the rectory door swings open disclosing Father Louis Reilly, St. Andrew's pastor, four hours late on his flight from Rome.

"Lou," his young assistant exclaims, "You had me worried. You okay?"

"You're up!" Father Lou says, genuinely surprised. "I didn't expect to see you at this hour."

"It was driving me crazy. The airline gave zero explanation, nothing. They just kept saying they had no information."

"We had to make an unscheduled landing, in Greenland. Some sort of equipment problem, I understand."

"Anyway, it's a Godsend to have you back," Father Tim says, grabbing his superior's bags.

They go into the kitchen. The young assistant heats up some cocoa he had had waiting on the stove.

"Did it wrap up okay over there?" he asked, pouring a cup for his boss.

"It's still going on. I had to plead hardship to get away. You don't need to be alone here."

"I didn't tell you the whole story. It wasn't just Felix's health."

"I'd heard."

"Yeah. Looking back, I think I could have handled it differently."

"Maybe so."

A pause, then Father Tim says, "I'll bet you're worn out."

"I'm fine. I dozed most of the way. But you should get some sleep."

Father Tim waves him off and breaks out into the broadest smile. "Lou, we've got a little surprise for you. Something from the parish."

Father Lou lets out a little chuckle, "What could that be?"

"We have a new roof."

"You're kidding."

"And it's paid for to the last nickel."

"How in heaven's name did we pull that off?"

"We had a parish drive. Everyone thought of it as a homecoming gift, but to be perfectly honest, Lou, penance may have had something to do with it, too, for that business with Felix."

"I need to hear more about that sometime. But right

now, young fellow, you need to turn in. And I'm taking the seven-thirty."

"No way. Not after coming halfway around the world."

"Tim, the seven-thirty is mine."

"Yes sir, boss. Right you are."

They both laugh. They get up and put cups into the sink.

As they pass his office, the young priest stops and says, "I got a gift too. Let me show you." He leads his boss into the office and points to the object on his desk.

"Recognize that?"

Father Lou bends over to inspect it. "It's Felix's cross. Did he give that to you?"

"No. I got it from someone he'd given it to. From that dazzler we talked about, Monica Trześniewska."

Father looks up, gazing more closely at his young assistant. He sees something never witnessed before.

"Is she still around?"

"She went off with a guy she knew from way back, a nice fellow with a last name almost as impossible as hers, Kwiatkowski. Jan Kwiatkowski. I married them two weeks ago. Monica joked she just might hyphenate her name."

"Amazing," the pastor says, struck by the news. He starts to chuckle. "Here we are in Rome wringing our hands over parish life, and all the good things are happening right here, in my own backyard no less."

Before they part, they exchange glances that are almost merry, two priests suddenly very happy in each other's presence.

"Get some sleep," Fr. Lou says. The young assistant nods and turns for his room, the older pastor to his.

The pastor is in no hurry to retire. He opens his bags and put shirts and socks back into the bureau, working slowly, rhythmically, one item at a time. Then he sets the alarm clock. It's the heart of the night, so still, so utterly quiet. So much has changed. He sinks down on the edge of his bed, more tired than he let on. He looks about him, then slowly, a blessed peace seeps into his weary frame, a special peace, a grace-filled peace, the kind of peace he knew only comes from long, heart-felt, finally answered prayer.

Epilogue

"

"

THIS POEM WAS FOUND AMONG THE EFFECTS of the late Rev. Felix Cooper. It is not known when the poem was written, or indeed whether the poem was ever addressed to a real person. Most likely it was written when he was quite young. If it was meant for a real person, it is not known who she might have been.

The kiss of your prayer for me
*   is closer than your lips*
*   more actual than your breath.*
When you whisper my name before God
*   you are mine more than I can dream.*
As for me, dear friend,
*   I am not yours until I am first all his.*